# The Green Machine

*Also by Michael Hardcastle*

## Motocross Stories

Fast From the Gate
Roar to Victory
Tiger of the Track

## Football Stories

Away From Home
Free Kick
Half a Team
Mascot
Soccer Special
The Team That Wouldn't Give In
United!

## Riding Stories

The Saturday Horse
The Switch Horse
Winning Rider

Caught Out    (A Cricket Story)
Rival Games   (An Athletics Story)
The Shooters   (A Netball Story)

MICHAEL HARDCASTLE

# The Green Machine

**MAMMOTH**

*Illustrated by Patrice Aitken*

First published in Great Britain 1989
by Methuen Children's Books Ltd

Published 1990 by Mammoth
an imprint of Mandarin Paperbacks
Michelin House, 81 Fulham Road, London SW3 6RB
Reprinted 1990

Mandarin is an imprint of the Octopus Publishing Group

Text copyright © 1989 Michael Hardcastle
Illustrations copyright © 1989 Patrice Aitken

ISBN 0 7497 0289 3

A CIP catalogue record for this title
is available from the British Library

Printed in Great Britain
by Cox and Wyman Ltd, Reading, Berkshire

# Contents

# One: A Free Offer

For several laps the man with all the money hadn't taken his eyes off Lee Parnaby. Now, as the riders soared over the last two jumps and then accelerated away from the tightest of the turns, he urged him on.

'Go on, son, go on! You can do it. YOU can get up into second place. Give it everything you've got!'

In fact, the man's voice didn't rise above a whisper. But even had he shouted Lee still wouldn't have been able to hear him over the roar of the engines, to say nothing of the frenzied yelling of some spectators who were related to other riders. The only sounds Lee could really hear were in his own mind: because he, too, was driving himself on to get a higher placing. His chance of victory had gone several laps earlier when he and his Honda had actually parted company. He'd come off when slewing across the track to avoid another rider and then been barged into by Greg Shearsmith. Luckily, neither he nor the Honda suffered any damage and he was back in the saddle in a matter of seconds. Nonetheless, his momentum had gone and it was another two laps before he could regain the position he held before the collision.

Greg, who also suffered in that encounter, had been having trouble since then with the engine of the ebony Shearsmith Special he was riding. The previous night his father, its designer, had carried out some last-minute refinements in the hope of getting an even better performance out of the machine that was the envy of so many of the members of the Skalbrooke Schoolpersons Motor-cycle Club. For once, though, that beautifully tuned engine wasn't functioning as intended.

With all his customary determination to get ahead and stay there, Greg flicked through the gears and changed his line of attack as he strove to overtake Lee, now holding third place in this Open Event on their home territory. Lee was equally intent on keeping Greg behind him. But not only that. His real aim was to pass the rider ahead of him. Second place wasn't as good as winning, of course, but it would represent a triumph after all the misfortune he'd experienced in the course of this motocross. On top of everything, it would mean he'd finish a long way in front of his brother, Darren. For Lee, there was always victory in that. Very little in life gave him more satisfaction than relegating his elder brother to a minor position.

As the double-S-bend came up for the last time Lee tilted his bike into the first turn, striving to save just a few centimetres of ground. He knew he was perilously close to the line of fluttering tape that marked the boundaries of the track. If he became entangled with that it could result in total disaster: tape that wrapped itself around the spokes of a rear wheel acted like a disc brake and the bike came instantaneously to a stop. By a margin no wider than a finger-nail, he managed to keep clear of that deadly tape. Through that bend he gained almost half a metre. And that was precious in his pursuit of the boy on the Kawasaki ahead of him.

Coming out of that first and sharpest turn his eye was caught by his cousin, Joanne, who had stationed herself so that he couldn't possibly miss seeing her: and Joanne was holding both index fingers up. They were placed side by side so as to form a simple signal: in effect, the number one. He couldn't acknowledge it because he needed both hands on the bike. But Joanne would know he'd got the message that he should be able to move up one position before the race ended. One of her great virtues was that there were times when she seemed able to read his mind and know exactly what he was thinking. It was uncanny.

He didn't know the identity of the boy on the Kawasaki but that didn't matter. His style was a low crouch, presumably to cut down wind resistance, and he seemed unafraid of anything. Lee sensed he wasn't going to be able to overtake him in so short a distance but he had to try. What he needed was some extra zip from the tank but, good though the Honda was, it couldn't provide miracles. When they reached the finishing straight he was flying – but still half-a-bike length behind his target. By now the winner had wheelied over the line to take the chequered flag and Lee experienced the usual pang of disappointment when he didn't win a race. He'd had his successes in recent months but he was eager to seize first place in every event.

After exchanging handshakes with the pair who'd beaten him ('Courtesy and consideration for others must be observed at all times', was one of the rules of the Club and the secretary insisted it be adhered to after a race as well as during it), he cruised into the paddock, stripping off his goggles as he went. The watcher in the red and green anorak nodded his satisfaction and decided to allow the boy a few moments to recover from the race before going to talk to him.

Joanne was waiting for Lee by the trailer in which the bikes were transported. 'Tenth,' she reported laconically and he didn't need to ask what she meant. Joanne was no fonder of Darren than he was.

'Just the right place for him. He's a tenth-rate rider,' Lee remarked, though there was no trace of bitterness in his tone.

There was a time, and it wasn't much more than a season or so earlier, when he'd found it impossible to complete a race in a higher position than his brother. But, in recent weeks, things had changed very much for the better. For some indefinable reason his own confidence had grown – and he believed it was nothing to do with the acquisition of a new bike, the fire-red Honda.

After months of indifference to her his liking for Joanne had built up to such an extent that he wanted to spend as much time as possible with her. She wasn't just his cousin, she had become his best friend, the person he could talk to about anything (well, he reflected, almost anything). She had always cared for him, he knew that, but she'd never forced her company upon him when he preferred to be on his own. Of course, it certainly helped their relationship that she was as eager to outwit Darren as he was.

'How far back was Greg?' he wanted to know. 'Did you see what he tried to do to me on Triangle Hill? Nearly knocked me out of the race completely!'

'Typical of him,' she replied, and tossed her head in just the way she used to do when her auburn hair reached to her shoulders. Now that it barely covered her ears the gesture looked more aggressive than graceful. 'Didn't do him any good, anyway. He sort of faded out in the last couple of hundred metres. Could be he's got engine trouble or was running out of juice. Maybe his fuel tank was *leaking*.'

Lee nodded thoughtfully. 'Could be. But it could be something else. I don't think the old Shearsmith Special is half as good as it used to be. Maybe Old Man Shearsmith is losing his touch at tuning up Greg's steed.'

Ever since an elderly spectator had been heard to comment that motocrossers resembled 'A bunch of wild cowboys, galloping their steeds all over the place', steed had become the in-word with the Skalbrooke riders. For weeks any use of it provoked instant hilarity and outsiders, of course, couldn't understand what was so funny.

'Lee, listen,' Joanne said fiercely. 'You know Dad's not going to be able to come back for us until ages after the meeting is over? Well, this is the great chance for me to do a couple of laps of the track on my own while everybody else is charging off home.'

Her pause was momentary. 'I mean, I can wear all your gear, can't I, because we're almost the same size? So even if anybody sees me they'll think it's you, having a bit of extra practice until Dad comes to collect the trailer. Is that OK?'

Lee felt he wasn't in a position to refuse. After all, it was Uncle Ken, Joanne's father, who owned the bikes, his and Darren's, and transported them to wherever they were racing. Ken Wragby still had the odd idea that girls weren't really intended to ride motorcycles in spite of the fact that the Skalbrooke Club had several schoolgirl members; Joanne herself had once been given a bike by her father as a belated birthday present but after wrecking it in an accident that wasn't her fault he'd decided that it was some sort of sign that she shouldn't be racing. What her father didn't know was that Joanne regularly practised on whatever bike she could get hold of whenever her father was out of sight and earshot. Although Lee tended to regard the new Honda as his own machine the truth was that it belonged to Joanne's father. On the other hand, he didn't want to risk upsetting his relationship with his uncle by helping Joanne to do something she wasn't supposed to do.

'Oh, come on, Lee,' she urged, trying to overcome his hesitation. 'You know how much I want to try out this new bike. You *know* I won't damage it or anything. I won't do any mad wheelies or *anything* stupid. So, come on, say I can!'

Still he hesitated. 'But, Jo, if . . . if . . . '

She pounced on what she believed was the difficulty. 'Oh, don't fuss about changing clothes! I won't look when you take your things off. You can just hand them out to me when you're in your usual gear. It's unbelievable how boys bother about things

13

like that! Anyway, we *are* related, you know, and I don't fuss about my – my *secrets* with you, do I?'

'Er, no,' he agreed. To his embarrassment she had touched upon one of the reasons for his reluctance to present her with the bike and everything else from his helmet and shoulder protectors to the reinforced smooth-soled boots. In truth, though, it wasn't the most important reason. 'It's Daz I'm worried about, Jo. If he finds out what we've done he'll go and cause trouble. Bound to. He'll be telling Uncle Ken about it in no time. And then, well . . . '

'Do you think I haven't thought about that?' she asked with some exasperation. 'He won't get in our way, I promise you. He's getting away from here as fast as he can, going off with that new pal of his.'

Lee frowned. 'New pal? Who's that?'

'Oh, I don't know his name! Does that matter? He's the one who's always going on about speedway and how fantastic it is and why don't we all turn into speedway stars and that sort of rubbish. Daz was taken in, naturally. Has to try something new when he can't succeed at what he's doing already. Look –'

'But, Jo, how do you know all this? I mean –'

'I just keep my ears and my eyes open, that's all. Simple really. Amazing what you can learn if you do that, Lee. You should try it some time.'

'No need to be sarcastic. I was just asking . . . '

'And I'm just asking to ride the family Honda,

that's all. I can't think why you're being so, so *unhelpful*. You know I'd always help you, with anything.'

Lee, still sitting astride the bike, now didn't know what to say. All his objections had been over-ruled. He knew very well that Joanne was a thoroughly capable rider.

If she was ever to persuade her father to allow her to compete again in real motocross events – which, Lee knew, was her greatest ambition – then she would have to prove right away that she was good enough to race against anybody. Merely taking part wouldn't be enough. Uncle Ken would be just as tough with her as he was with his nephews when he was in a demanding mood.

'OK, then – ' he was starting to say when a tall man with a mass of gingery hair, wearing a red and green anorak suddenly arrived beside them. He smiled politely as if waiting for them to finish their conversation. Then, aware of the surprise he'd caused, he started speaking.

'Hope you don't mind my butting in but I'd be most grateful if I could have a word with you, Lee,' he began in a smooth, cultured voice. 'It is a matter of some, shall we say, importance. Oh, and very much to your advantage, I imagine.'

Lee was astonished. He couldn't imagine what on earth this beaming, friendly figure wanted with him;

he wasn't anyone Lee had seen at a previous motocross event.

'Is this, er, private, you know, just between the two of you?' asked Joanne, quick as always to react to a new situation. 'I mean, I'll push off if you want so – '

'No, no!' Lee said hurriedly. Unexpected approaches from over-friendly strangers were always to be treated with suspicion, he'd once been told. Joanne's presence was especially welcome at this moment. 'Er, this is my cousin, Joanne. Her dad – he's around here somewhere – looks after our bikes. I mean – '

'And bikes, or rather, one motorbike in particular, is what I want to talk to you about, Lee,' the man told him, his smile not wavering for an instant. 'I expect you are very attached to your Honda and it looks a nice machine. But I can offer you something much, much better. A bike that will take you straight to the front, to the very top if you like, and keep you there. Now – '

'My dad's just bought Lee that bike,' Joanne broke in, pointing to the Honda he was still straddling, 'so I can promise you he won't be willing to fork out for another new bike for, oh, for *years*. So – '

'Hey, hey, hold on!' the man cut back. 'I haven't said a single word about *buying* anything. I'm not here to sell. I'm here to provide you with something that's absolutely free, no strings attached, no hidden clauses – er, motives. A gift. Just for you, Lee, A brand new bike with all the spares and equipment you'll ever need. So, what do you say to that, eh?'

# Two: Best in the World?

Lee didn't say anything for some moments but his face reflected the emotions chasing through his mind. Neither Joanne, also looking bewildered, nor the stranger tried to speed up his response.

Eventually, he muttered, almost aggressively: 'I don't believe it.'

The man laughed. 'D'you know, son, I had a bet with myself that you'd say exactly that! Well, I suppose that's inevitable because – '

'Look, I don't like being called son,' Lee interrupted. 'My name's Lee, OK?'

'Oh, sorry. Sure, whatever you like. But doesn't your dad call you son at any time?'

'My dad's at sea – he works on a ship – so he's not usually around to call me anything. Look, what's the catch about this bike offer? I'm not getting mixed up in anything that's, well, dicey.'

Suddenly the man stepped forward and thrust out his hand which Lee shook a trifle reluctantly.

'Sorry, Lee, I should have introduced myself properly. Mike Martin, that's my name, and I'm the regional promotions manager for Namura, the world's newest and most advanced motocross bike. You probably haven't heard of us yet but soon every rider in the land will be wishing he was lined up at the starting gate on a Namura. Within a couple of years we plan to capture a huge share of the market. Lee, I promise you: Namura riders will be on a winner!'

Lee could sense that the man was speaking in publicity slogans but that didn't curtail his interest in what he was hearing. Namura certainly was a new name to him and that made it all the more interesting because every motocrosser was keen to acquire a better bike.

'So you're going to give me one of these bikes, just like that, just to ride in every race I'm in?' asked Lee, trying to keep the sarcasm as mild as possible.

'Exactly!' agreed Mike Martin, nodding vigorously. 'We want you to demonstrate the great qualities of this computer-designed bike in this area, and wherever else you go racing. If you come up against another Namura demonstration model ridden by another of our chosen people, well, that's fine. Everybody'll be able to see how terrific they are because we reckon they'll probably finish in the first two places! That's how confident we are of our product, Lee.'

Lee glanced across at Joanne. But for once she was paying little attention to him, appearing lost in her own thoughts.

'Why have you picked me – to give the bike to, I mean?' he asked. 'I'm not a regular winner, you know. This afternoon I even fell off and – '

' – And you got straight back on and rode like a demon,' Mr Martin added, nodding approvingly. 'I was watching, son – Lee – and I was very impressed by your style, your determination, just about everything you did. Look, this isn't the first time I've seen you in action. I was at Tockington the other week when you took the Open there in great style. You're a great one for coming up from way back, aren't you? I imagine most people had written you off after you got caught up in that huge maul down in the ravine. But you just pushed that to the back of your mind, didn't you, and got your head down and, boy, did you fly at the end!'

Lee was impressed. Of course, he'd had no idea anyone was studying him so closely at the Tockington track. But then, when he was racing all that mattered to him was his performance in the race itself. He was never aware of mere spectators. It was also true, as Mr Martin had guessed, that he didn't allow mishaps to affect his concentration if he still had a chance of victory.

'Well, thanks,' was all he could think to say in response to such praise.

'By the way, I'd better tell you that we don't take these decisions just on our own at Namura,' Mike Martin pointed out. 'I had a colleague with me at Tockington, our sales director as it happens, and he has a high opinion of your skills – and your potential for doing even better in future. I remember he also thought you remained very calm when things might easily have gone wrong for you. Remaining calm under pressure is a great asset, Lee.'

'But I can also get mad,' Lee said, beginning to grin.

Mr Martin's own smile was on full beam again. 'I'm sure you can! But that, too, can work to your advantage under, er, certain circumstances. There are times when everyone's got to get fired up. Otherwise you'll just, well, let rivals drive right over you, and that's no good in a motocross rider. It's a great sport but you've got to be competitive to survive. Now – '

'Look, do you ever give your bikes to girls?' asked Joanne, who'd moved across to stand beside Lee, her fingers trailing loosely along the length of the handlebars of the Honda.

'Er, I don't think we have, not yet.' Mike Martin looked very surprised by that question. 'But, well, it wouldn't be impossible, not if we found the right girl rider.'

Joanne seemed to be on the verge of saying something else; but then she deliberately bit her lip and remained silent until Lee said what was on his mind.

'When do I get to see this new bike?'

'Ah, that means you'd like to accept our offer, does it, Lee?' The smile, if anything, was broader than ever.

'Depends. I mean, I like my Honda, I've had some good races on it. Never let me down. So, first, I'd want to see if your bike is as good – well, better than the Honda. Otherwise, there's no point in changing, is there?'

'Good thinking, Lee, I knew we'd made the right choice in you. It's absolutely essential that you believe, you *feel*, that our machine is the best in the world, the best you could *ever* sit on.' Mike paused after that further burst of enthusiasm. When he spoke again he pitched his voice at a much lower level as if afraid of being overheard by spies. 'The bike is under wraps at the moment. It's not due to be launched on the market just yet. So when it is, we have to make a big publicity splash about it. Understand?'

Lee nodded. 'You mean it's on the secret list?'

'Right! Of course, there've been rumours about it, and lots of people know our name because of our other products, but hardly anybody's seen the bike in action yet, apart from our own engineers and sales force. I can promise you, Lee, you'll be one of the first young riders in Britain ever to ride a Namura!'

Lee's interest in the new bike was growing visibly and now Joanne was regarding him with some awe; her other emotions she was just managing to keep in check for the present.

'So when do I get to see this bike?' Lee asked for the second time.

'What we've got to do is to arrange a trial ride for you on our private circuit as soon as possible,' Mike said quietly, then glanced behind him as if he still feared that someone was eavesdropping on their talk. 'Look, when I can arrange to see your folks to fix up – '

'It's my dad you need to see,' Joanne broke in hastily. 'He's the one who's in charge of the bikes and everything for Lee and Darren – Darren's Lee's elder brother, by the way. Dad won't be back for, oh, another hour but you could phone us up tonight to sort things out. I'll give you the number. I'm sure Dad will be really interested in your new bike for Lee. I expect he'll jump at the chance of a new machine because motocross costs him a fantastic amount of money. He's always saying that.'

'Well, in that case, I will contact your dad,' Mike said, sounding rather dubious about the prospect. Producing his pocket notebook, he jotted down Ken Wragby's address and telephone number. 'Look, I'll be in touch as soon as possible – probably tonight. We want to get things fixed up without any delay. Is there any particular date when you wouldn't be free to do the trial? Any commitments that would keep you late at school, for instance? That sort of thing.'

Lee shook his head. 'Can't think of any. Oh, yes, I go to karate classes on Tuesday evenings – wouldn't want to miss them.'

Mike Martin's eyebrows had shot up on hearing that, so Joanne rushed in again to explain. 'Lee started to learn karate so that he could defend himself after he'd been beaten up in mistake for Daz – Darren, I mean. Now he's *really* an expert, aren't you, Lee?'

When Lee merely frowned as if he hadn't wanted such information to be disclosed Mike nodded his approval. 'Good to hear, that. You've obviously got the right attitude, Lee. I'm very impressed – just as you'll be impressed by our *sensational* Namura! OK, then, I'll be in touch. Meanwhile, not a word to anyone else about our agreement.'

Lee waited until Mike was out of earshot before muttering: 'Didn't know I'd actually *agreed* anything, except to – '

'Fabulous, fabulous, FABULOUS!' Joanne was now exclaiming at practically the top of her voice, not listening to a word that Lee was saying. He was amazed. His cousin had never been the demonstrative type in his experience.

'What are you going *on* about?' he asked when she calmed down enough to be able to hear him.

Now she looked astonished. 'What do you mean,

Lee? Why aren't *you* overjoyed at the chance of riding a fabulous new bike? I just think it's, well, wonderful for you!'

'But we don't really know it's going to be fabulous, do we?' Lee pointed out. 'I mean, every manufacturer will always want to boost his own thing, won't he, even if it's no good at all? Mike Martin's bound to claim that this Namura is the best in the world because he wants to sell it to everybody. It could turn out to be a load of rubbish.'

Joanne was exasperated by his caution. 'Oh, come on, Lee! Show *some* enthusiasm. I think it's great that Namura have chosen *you* to be one of their riders. Honestly, it's a great compliment. I can tell you one thing for sure: Daz will be hopping mad! He'll never get over this, you being chosen ahead of him.'

'Yes, there is that,' agreed Lee, brightening.

'Well, I'm going to celebrate,' Joanne announced. 'You said I could have a go on the Honda so hand it over. Time's getting short and Dad could be back almost any time.'

Lee wasn't sure that he had said she could ride the Honda but he wasn't in a mood to argue. His mind was now on other matters. Handing over his helmet and gloves, he collected his ordinary clothes from the locker in the trailer and then began to remove his leather riding gear, back- and shoulder-protectors and everything else that Joanne would need. True to her word, she kept out of sight while he changed though, rather suspiciously, she re-appeared the very instant he was ready to hand the items to her. She'd already stripped off her outer clothing and was now revealed in T-shirt and quite dazzling red shorts.

'You're improving,' she told him with a typical slightly mocking grin. 'You don't look embarrassed this time!'

'There's nothing to be embarrassed about,' Lee said a little pompously, watching as his cousin swiftly zipped herself into his precious riding kit. Even the boots appeared to fit perfectly. 'Look, take care, won't you?'

'Are you thinking about me or the bike or the gear?' she inquired before putting the red and white helmet on.

'Oh, er, everything,' he replied diplomatically. Fleetingly he wondered whether to issue a warning about the state of the stutter bumps on the lower part of the circuit but thought better of it. After all, she always seemed to assume that he knew exactly what he was doing whether he was practising or competing.

She rode away with complete assurance: no attempt to show off, no erratic gear changes, just neatly and positively, heading for an opening close to the first S-bend. The track was deserted and even the paddock was emptying rapidly of vans and trailers, converted buses and shiny station wagons. Lee supposed they ought to have asked permission of the club secretary or some other official for Joanne to do her practice lap but, of course, that would have given the game away: that the rider in the red and white helmet wasn't Lee Parnaby, an official member of the club and thus entitled to ask for practice time, but a girl called Joanne Wragby who was only a relative of a member. That reminded him that perhaps he ought to keep out of sight in case –

'Hey, I thought I saw you zooming over the saddle jump just now!' said an all too familiar voice, cutting into his thoughts. Lee's heart lurched as he turned to see his uncle's head thrust through the open driver's window of his red Ford saloon.

'Oh, hello, Uncle Ken! Sorry, I didn't see – I mean hear – you coming up . . . .'

'Not surprised. You were day-dreaming, Lee, day-dreaming. No doubt about that. It *is* your bike out there, isn't it? I mean, I only caught a glimpse over the fence as I drove down Tellman Hill but I think I can spot that bike a mile off now.'

If Joanne was already over the saddle jump then it wouldn't be more than a few moments before she came into sight again along the finishing straight. The question would be answered then so there was no point in delaying the inevitable.

'Yeah, it's my bike,' he admitted, thinking that he

28

could just as easily have said 'your' bike. He knew very well what the next question would be so there was no point in not adding: 'Joanne's having a go on it.'

He waited for the explosion.

Instead, Ken Wragby simply looked mildly surprised and he even managed a smile: a faint smile but a smile nonetheless. What Lee didn't know was that his uncle had just had a meeting with the boss of his company and been given some excellent news: he was being promoted and thus would earn a higher salary and qualify for a higher rate of bonuses. In a way, it was as much his lucky day as it was Lee's, although Lee still hadn't realised that he was in luck.

Joanne came into sight. Lee knew that she must have noticed her father's arrival and so he expected her to pull off the track. She'd want to explain exactly what she'd been up to and doubtless hope to be forgiven. But, with a wave in their direction, she rode on, standing well clear of the saddle as she negotiated a couple of minor bumps before settling down to ride determinedly into the first steep curve at the start of another circuit.

'Looks good,' Uncle Ken commented to Lee's increasing amazement. 'She was well balanced there. Showed economy, too, on that bend. Yes, pretty good.'

Lee risked an observation of his own. 'I thought

you didn't approve of girls riding in motocross. Well, Joanne, anyway.'

Uncle Ken shrugged. 'Oh well, it's not always a good thing to hold people back when they're keen on something. Joanne's kept up her interest in this game longer than I ever thought she would. I imagined she'd grow out of it and want to go in for ice-skating or playing the flute or something of that nature. Doesn't seem she's going to, however.'

The laugh with which Lee greeted that remark caused his uncle to give him a sharp look. 'I was just thinking that if Jo went in for music she'd probably play the drums or a trumpet, not a flute!'

Ken Wragby shared his amusement. 'You're probably right, Lee. She's capable of making quite a noise these days when she's in the mood.'

Moments later Joanne made an appropriately loud return to the paddock, revving the engine in joyous fashion as she became aware of the smile on her father's face. It wouldn't have surprised her if it had been dark with rage.

'Hey,' she exclaimed, the instant she'd whipped off Lee's helmet. 'Has he told you the great news? The *fantastic* news!' She sensed she must make the most of her father's obvious good mood.

When, looking suitably puzzled, he shook his head, Joanne rushed on: 'Then go on, Lee, tell him! Tell him about Mr Martin's great offer.'

His uncle listened attentively without interrupting once as Lee recounted all the details of their conversation with Mike Martin. His expression didn't really alter from start to finish and Lee's hopes that Uncle Ken would find no fault with the offer grew anew.

'Well, sounds like a pretty good arrangement to me, especially if Namura are going to provide all the spares and any extra equipment we need,' Mr Wragby said approvingly when Lee finished. 'It'll certainly save me a load of money if everything really does work in our favour. Yes, I think we should definitely give it a go, Lee.'

'Great! Thanks, Uncle. So when – '

'But one thing you didn't mention,' Mr Wragby went on. 'How does Darren fit into all this? Does he get one of these bikes, too?'

Lee and his cousin exchanged hurried glances and it was Joanne who answered. 'Daz isn't included, Dad. Mr Martin just wants Lee because he thinks Lee has loads of potential. Daz hasn't exactly been leading the charge lately, has he?'

'No, true,' her father said reflectively, 'but I've always treated you two boys the same and it's not going to seem fair to Darren if you get something he hasn't got. I mean, I got you the new Honda, Lee, because your brother had his new bike last season. Now – '

'Uncle, could you do something for me, *please*? Don't tell Daz about this, not yet. I know he's going to be mad, I know he's going to be jealous. Bound to be. That's Daz. So *please* could we not tell him until after the trial ride's over and I either have this new bike or I don't?'

The plea was so fervently expressed that Ken Wragby hadn't the heart to turn it down, even though he suspected that he was being unfair to his elder nephew. But Lee really was the better, the more adventurous, rider of the two and so he deserved his chance of further success with this new model. Moreover, after his own success with his boss he was in an indulgent mood.

'OK,' he agreed. 'But it won't be easy keeping it a secret from him for long. In any case, he's got to be told, he's *entitled* to be told, when the trial's over and it's been decided which bike you'll ride in future, Lee. That's only fair.'

Another thought had struck Lee. 'When Mr Martin gets in touch with you could you please make sure that he doesn't call for me when Daz is likely to be around. I mean I could – '

'But Lee, you'll be coming to our house so that Mr Martin can pick us all up together,' Joanne pointed out. 'Daz won't need to know where you are then or where you're going.'

'Oh yes, of course,' admitted Lee, feeling distinctly foolish. His anxiety to prevent his brother from meeting the Namura people seemed to be affecting his intelligence. But he knew that Darren, as soon as he heard about the new bike, would do everything possible to get one for himself. If that was impossible then his jealousy would be such that he'd probably try to get Namura's offer to Lee withdrawn. To Darren any advantage won by his younger brother would be intolerable.

'So, as soon as we've heard from this Namura man and got a date fixed I'll give you a ring, Lee, and then we'll take it from there,' Uncle Ken promised.

Joanne was still in a state of ecstasy. 'Oh, it's so exciting!' she exclaimed, as she wheeled the Honda up to the trailer so that they could start their preparations for leaving the track. 'Exciting for *everybody* in the family – but especially for you, Lee.'

'I know,' Lee replied. But his tone suggested that he still didn't really believe that at the next Skalbrooke meeting he'd be riding the world's latest superbike.

# Three:   Secret Trials

'Here we go then,' announced Mike Martin, braking smoothly and then steering the car into the narrow space beside the cabin occupied by security guards. Ahead of them was the barrier with the Stop Here pole still in place. Even though, as the company's regional promotions manager, Martin must have been a familiar figure to the guards on duty, that pole wasn't going to be raised to allow them to drive in until he and his guests had been given official clearance to proceed.

'I didn't really expect it to be like this,' remarked Joanne from the back seat as she surveyed the electrified fence and the powerful arc lamps that were angled to illuminate it. 'Bit like a prison camp, really. Oh, sorry, Mr Martin, I didn't mean – '

'Don't apologise, Joanne,' said Mr Martin as he drove through the barrier and headed for a distant building. 'In an industry like ours we have to protect our secrets as securely as a gaol guards its prisoners.

Trade secrets are just as valuable as, well, as gold bricks. If you don't look after 'em someone from the opposition will try to pinch 'em. Then you'll find they come up with a carbon copy of something you've invested millions in, millions of pounds and millions of man-hours of research. It's called industrial espionage. Sophisticated phrase really for common robbery.'

Lee was no less impressed by the sheer size of the Namura site. It had never occurred to him that the manufacturing units would be so huge nor that the offices would be contained in a tall, elegant octagonal structure that seemed to be made made mainly of black glass and shiny steel. The building they were now approaching was isolated from the rest and beyond it all he could see was rugged, open land with scattered vegetation: ideal motocross country, in his view.

'Right,' Mike exclaimed, slapping Lee on the shoulder as they left the car. 'You'll be in action in no time. I hope this is going to be a day you'll never forget, the day you rode your first Namura XU, the day – '

'What's XU stand for?' interrupted Joanne.

Mike grinned. 'Knew you wouldn't be able to resist asking that! I have the firmest idea that you like to know the details of everything that's going on around you, and then some. XU means Extra Universal, which roughly translated stands for "Can go over everything in the whole world, and then some." OK?'

They were met at the entrance to the long, low building by two men, one already dressed to ride in a gleaming blue leather suit adorned with a variety of company logos and motor trade symbols, the other tall, thin, grey-suited, whom Mike introduced as his boss; which greatly surprised Joanne, for one, because he looked even younger than Martin himself. The boss enthusiastically shook hands with them all and then told them what was about to happen.

'We'll be rolling out a couple of test bikes in a moment and Emilio here,' indicating the man in blue leathers, 'will give you a lead round the circuit, Lee. He'll keep an eye on you in case you need any advice – don't suppose a boy of your experience will, though. So he'll be ready to drop back and ride alongside if you need him to. Then you're on your own. Just do what you want. The track's not a crazy one or anything like that. Just got enough kinks in it to bring out the best in you – and the bike. How's that sound, son? Oh, sorry, *Lee*. Mike tells me you like your name ahead of anything else. Quite right. I'm the same. I've always preferred Simon to being Mr Barrow or SB. Hope you'll call me that, too.'

'Great, I'm looking forward to it,' Lee said, and then his eyes widened as two emerald green motorcycles with white saddles and white sidewall tyres, piloted by men in mechanic's overalls, cruised into view from behind the far end of the building.

'Hey, that's a really fabulous colour combination!' Joanne exclaimed. 'I hadn't expected it to be green. I mean – '

'Sure, it surprises almost everyone,' Simon agreed. 'Yeah, we all know Kawasakis are usually green, too, but that's a sort of lime colour, isn't it? Ours is real emerald, just like the jewel. Which is what our bike is. When we first worked on the plans our code name for it was simply The Green Machine. We knew if we got it right it would turn every other manufacturer green with envy! And I know from the reactions from the trade so far that we weren't far wrong.'

By now Lee at last had his hands on the Namura. It was the sleekest, most handsome machine he'd ever seen and he was impatient to try it out (impatience was one of Daz's faults but Lee wasn't thinking about him now). First, though, Simon wanted to extol some of the bike's greatest virtues and, particularly, its braking system (the very latest design of discs front and rear) and explosive acceleration.

Lee, who'd travelled in his riding gear, was all set to ride off when his uncle asked what he regarded as a crucial question. 'Just one thing, Simon: what about insurance on this, er, test run? And in the future? I mean – '

Simon held up both hands like someone surrendering. 'Everything's been taken care of in that direction, I assure you, Mr Wragby. Part of the company's policy is to insure bike as well as rider for the first year of their partnership. The bike itself is as indestructible as any bike could be. We think the only possible problem could be if some foreign substance is introduced into the fuel system. Naturally, we can't control what people put into a bike but . . . You'd have to be crazy to wreck a Namura, I reckon.'

The rest of the conversation Lee didn't hear. Already he was on the move, following in Emilio's track as precisely as he could. The first gradient was still some way off and he wondered what sort of obstacles the circuit would contain. He'd been rather surprised they hadn't told him what to look out for; but then he rationalised that they would deliberately want him to take each obstacle as it came so that he would find out what the bike was like. Everything about it was pleasing him so far, from its glossy appearance to the recessed grooves for the safety wires on the handgrips. On a previous machine he'd actually got blisters on his thumb because of the awkwardness of the grip.

They were speeding up. Suddenly Emilio zoomed ahead. When Lee went for the same acceleration he found the response breathtaking. 'Wow!' he told himself – and then positioned himself for the jump that came up over the lip of the sharp ascent.

Suddenly the track became a tightly linked chain of bends and curves and Lee needed maximum concentration to make sure he didn't lose touch with his leader. There was one hill that looked to be almost vertical as they swung into it from an innocuous sloping right-hander.

Lee sucked in breath – and went for it. The bike soared like a bird. It was all so effortless he was hardly aware of tackling such a formidable gradient. Emilio was now glancing back with a hint of concern but Lee simply gave him a wave and then powered after him. From then on they were racing. Lee didn't manage to catch him up but the gap between them was insignificant when they completed the oval trip.

'So, what's the verdict?' Simon wanted to know when Lee killed the engine.

'Brilliant, absolutely brilliant!' was the answer. Lee wasn't exaggerating.

'Well, you certainly looked good, the two of you together, you and the green machine,' Mike Martin added. 'Didn't you think so, Joanne?'

'Oh, yes, wonderful,' she agreed instantaneously. Then, with one of her mocking grins she added: 'But I shouldn't have said that, really, because I'm speechless – speechless with envy. Or do I mean jealousy?'

That provoked the laugh she'd intended it to but Mike sensed the meaning behind the remark.

'Would you like to have a go on it as well, Joanne? I remember your saying something to me last Sunday about girls riding our bikes. And so far we haven't had the pleasure of watching a girl in action on a Namura, have we, Simon?'

'That's right,' said his boss. 'Sure, have a spin, Joanne. Oh, and maybe we should get a photo of you afterwards when you've taken all that gear off. Be a good thing for our publicity department to show that pretty girls ride our bikes!'

Her prayer, as well as her ploy, had been answered! Joanne, aware that both her father and Lee were now looking intently at her for different reasons, could tell what her cousin was thinking. She was wearing jeans and a light sweater and Lee wouldn't want to hand over all his protective clothing in front of everyone else. But . . .

'But she's not wearing the right gear,' her father pointed out. 'So – '

'Oh, don't worry about that, Mr Wragby,' Mike cut in. 'We can kit her out with everything she needs. If we can't, our promotions department isn't as good as I keep telling everyone it is!'

It was hard to tell who was the more relieved to hear that offer, Lee or Joanne. Then, while she was taken off to be fitted out, the men began to discuss the finer details of the company's manufacturing processes. Lee, who could never get excited about such technical matters, began to imagine what it would be like to race his new bike in the fiercest competition. There was a Challenge Cup Meeting at Kingskettle the following Monday, a Bank Holiday. Would the Namura be his by then?

All the time at the back of his mind was the worry of how Darren would react to the news of his new possession. He had no doubt at all that Daz would protest at maximum volume. Yet Lee had the distinct impression these days that Uncle Ken was getting a bit fed up with Darren's antics and attitudes. Because Darren was the elder, by exactly one year and one day, he believed that he was entitled to be first in everything in family and social matters. Therefore he was bound to argue that if a new bike was available then it should be given to him.

But Lee was going to insist, whether Uncle Ken supported him or not, that the bike had been offered to him and him alone because of the skills he'd displayed and what Namura described as his 'potential'. He was positive that if the Namura people saw Daz in action on the track they wouldn't be impressed at all – and they'd surely take a dim view of the sort of rotten tricks he got up to in order to improve his chances in a race.

When Joanne re-emerged in the company of Mike Martin there was a spontaneous round of applause from the assembled watchers. In keeping with the company's colour scheme she was dressed in green and white: green riding suit, white gloves and white helmet. Lee was still surprised that her father hadn't said anything about his not approving of girls riding in motocross. So perhaps, at last, he was going to allow her to compete again.

Certainly no one could fault her style or performance the Namura. Once again, Emilio led the way but Lee suspected that he wasn't setting quite the pace that he, Lee, had responded to; possibly he'd been told by Simon Barrow to take things easy in case the girl was inexperienced or lacked confidence.

'You know, if we had another spare bike I really think we might be offering it to you, young lady,' Simon greeted her on her return.

Joanne immediately shot a look at her father. His expression was thoughtful. But he reacted quickly enough to say: 'Well done, Joanne.'

That was pallid, however, compared to Lee's: 'Great ride, Jo! You looked really good. Hey, it's a terrific machine, isn't it?'

So, with everyone apparently agreed on everything to do with the Namura offer, the men went off to sign formal documents about the conditions of the Agreement. Lee was a little disappinted to discover that his signature wasn't needed because he was too young. But he could console himself with the thought that the gleaming green and white machine really was his now; so his chances of winning important races had been given a tremendous boost. That prospect sent a tingle of excitement right through him.

'I know just what *you're* thinking,' Joanne claimed when she returned from handing in her kit at the promotions office.

He duly confirmed it. 'You don't blame me, do you?'

Joanne shook her head. 'Course not. So what's going to happen to your *nearly* new Honda now?'

'Don't really know. But I *suppose* Darren'll get it. That'll – '

'Not if I can help it,' his cousin interrupted forcefully. 'I want it and I'm going to have it!'

Lee registered all the disbelief he was experiencing. 'But you know Uncle Ken doesn't think girls should race. He's said so plenty of times. And you know Daz will go mad if he misses out. He thought he should have the new Honda even though *he* got a new bike *last* season. So – '

'Look, just back me up when I talk to dad, OK?' Joanne murmured as the men came towards them still in a rainbow of smiles.

There were handshakes all round and lots of expressions of goodwill and confidence in the outcome of the new partnership. The company photographer who'd already shot pictures of Joanne astride the bike now snapped some more of those handshakes and smiles.

'It's a bit like winning the pools,' Lee whispered to Joanne. 'Except this is better because we didn't even have to enter to win this bike!'

As soon as Mike Martin, after repeating the company's promise that the new bike would be delivered within seventy-two hours, tuned up and ready to race, had dropped them off at Joanne's home she tackled her dad about the Honda.

'I'd like it, Dad. Please can I have it? *Please*.'

Ken Wragby looked startled. 'Well, I was thinking that perhaps Darren – '

'Daz has got a bike, a new one, the one you gave him last season; Lee has got a new bike, the new Namura. So the Honda will be spare. And I *haven't* got a bike. And you know I can ride OK, you saw it today and everybody, *everybody*, all those experts like Mr Barrow and Mike Martin and, oh what's his name, yeah, *Emilio*, they *all* said I rode well. And that if they had another spare bike, another spare Namura, then they'd let me – '

'Hold on, Joanne, for goodness' sake slow down!' her father pleaded. He'd never heard her go on like this about anything: this waterfall of words, this passionate entreaty. Lee was equally surprised. But he felt there was nothing he could say that would aid Joanne's cause. She was perfectly capable of winning on her own.

'But running *three* bikes in the family is going to cost me a heck of a lot of extra money even if

46

Namura *are* paying for any spares and – '

But he couldn't say any more because Joanne knew she had won; and so she flung herself into his arms to hug and kiss him.

'Thank you, thank you, thank you,' she exulted after detaching herself at last. 'I won't let you down. I really do know how to ride, you know.'

'I do know,' her father admitted, to the astonishment of the cousins. 'I actually saw you riding at Skalbrooke last season when you thought I wasn't around. You'd borrowed Darren's bike when he'd gone off with one of his mates.'

'And you never said a word!' Joanne exclaimed, almost accusingly.

'Deliberately. I wanted to find out if you were just playing around or whether you were still serious, whether you *cared* enough to keep riding. Sometimes, you know, your dad's not as dim as you seem to think he is. I *do* notice what's going on around me.'

'Oh,' was the only response Joanne could come up with; but then her eagerness to set wheels in motion resurfaced. 'So can I ride at Kingskettle on Monday with Lee – oh, and Daz? Could you ring the club secretary to fix up membership and stuff like that? Then the Saturday after that there's our own Open meeting – well, it's two days, isn't it? I really want to do well in that, show guys like Greg Shearsmith and Nathan Pike that I'm just as good as them. And Lee, too, of course!'

Lee had no doubt at all that she would be a tough opponent on the track but he merely raised his eyebrows and returned her grin.

'Well, I'm not sure about that one, Joanne.' Mr Wragby reached into an inner pocket for some papers he'd been given by the Namura people. He studied one of the pages. 'Yes, that's the weekend Lee's got to race at a very special meeting at Taplow Castle – that's over one hundred miles from here and we'll be staying the weekend. Well, the riders will. They – Namura – think it's a perfect opportunity to show off the bike in competition. So that meeting's going to have to come first.'

'But that's OK, I can ride there, too,' Joanne said breezily, expecting now that everything would work in her favour. 'I mean, it'll be a good opportunity for me, too, to get experience of another track. Great!'

'Look, don't rush things, Jo,' her father warned. 'The invitation is for Lee, no one else. I've already been thinking about Darren, wondering how he's going to take it if I can't swing an invitation for him. He's not going to like it one little bit if I can't do things for him.'

'Don't I know it, murmured Lee.

# Four:  Tricky Terrain

Of course, Darren was furious: furious that Lee had been chosen ahead of him to ride the Namura; furious that Joanne was to have the Honda; furious that he might not be included in the invitations to the Taplow Castle Special Motocross.

It was Lee who'd given him the news, something Uncle Ken had admitted he was thankful to avoid. Lee hadn't minded because he was quite happy to watch Daz get mad to no avail. His brother really looked funny when he lost his temper: his face reddened, he actually appeared to spit as he shouted and he clenched his fist so hard the knuckles whitened. Lee had hugged the news to himself for several days, not releasing it until they were due to set off for Uncle Ken's on the morning of the Kingskettle meeting. It was his theory that Daz's anger wouldn't die down for the whole day and therefore it would affect his riding and his judgment. After all their battles down the years Lee was willing to seize any advantage he could spot.

'How could they possibly pick on *you* to show off a bike?' Darren wailed for the umpteenth time as they reached the end of their journey, parking their push bikes behind the garage.

'Told you, they can see into the future, they know I'm going to the top. They also like the fact that I'm *calm* in a crisis. Not like you, Daz: you blow up, like a flaming volcano, if the slightest thing bothers you. You – '

'That's just adrenalin – getting the adrenalin flowing. If you know so much, little brother, you should know that every top sportsman needs to get up a bit of steam to perform at his best. And I can be patient – and patience counts.'

Lee had never heard a more unbelievable claim. 'You, patient! You go at everything like a crazy bull, rushing – '

'Then how do you think I catch so many deep-sea fish, eh? Tell me that, Lee-tle one! You only catch fish out there if you're as patient as – as a saint. And you know I catch those fish because you help to eat 'em.'

'I didn't know you *caught* them. I thought they just died of shock on catching sight of your ugly mug!'

Darren was just on the point of swinging a punch (which Lee had predicted and was ready to evade) when Joanne darted round the corner of the house.

'Hey, you two, cut it out! Honestly, talk about brotherly love . . . .'

'You, you've got my bike!' Darren accused her. 'Come on, hand it over. It's supposed to be mine and – '

'*Supposed*? Supposed nothing,' Joanne shot back at him. 'It actually belongs to my dad and he gave it to *me*. So I'm riding it every race there is from now on, Darren Daniel Parnaby!'

'Girls can't ride motocross, never could,' sneered D.D. Parnaby. 'When did you last see a girl win a race?'

'Natalie Carlyle, three weeks ago,' was the prompt answer. 'So there!'

'That was just a fluke because most of us were in a pile up caused by some idiot who couldn't steer a pram on a pavement! And in the next race she fell off at the first bend. Just shows you. Girls can't ride motocross.'

'Well, you'd better watch out, Dazzer, because Joanne here is better than you already. I know, I've seen her ride.'

'Oh, typical of you to side with the girls! Well, that's where you ought to stay, in the *girls'* room where they'll show you what – '

It was the arrival of Uncle Ken that arrested him in mid-attack. He swallowed hard and he glowered but he shut up. Ken Wragby was, naturally, well aware of the rivalry between his nephews but he felt it was best ignored, so long as he treated them equally in practically every respect. From time to time he deferred to Darren simply because Darren demanded to be recognised as the elder brother who was entitled to extra privileges because of that seniority. That was why, when he could afford to replace bikes or racing equipment, Ken Wragby tended to give Darren's needs precedence. Now, however, the choice of who should come first had been made by others: senior executives of the Namura Motorcycle Company. All the same, he felt a tinge of sympathy for Darren's apparent demotion.

'All right then, Darren?' he inquired cheerfully. He sensed he'd interrupted an argument between the three of them but that he ignored, too. They could settle that when they were on their own again. 'Ready to pick up a trophy or two today, then?'

'Might be, if I had a brand-new, computer-designed superbike to ride, like someone we all know who doesn't deserve it,' was the churlish response. 'Or even a new-season's Honda.'

Mr Wragby suddenly felt annoyed. 'Look, Darren, it was the Namura people who chose Lee, who offered him their new bike. It was entirely their decision. I chose to let Joanne have the Honda because I think she deserves the chance to ride in competition. She's been very supportive of you boys and never – well, hardly ever – asked for anything for herself. In the past I've always done my best for you and I'll go on doing that as long as I can. Frankly, your attitude does you no credit. You're just being unfair to everyone.'

For once Darren looked guilty. 'Sorry, Uncle,' he somehow found the grace to say.

Normally when they travelled to a meeting Darren insisted on sitting in the front passenger seat but this time it was clear he wanted to sit in the back. He lost out on that, too, because Lee and Joanne dived on to the back seat the moment the car was out of the garage. So the journey to the workshop to collect the bikes and the trailer was heavy with silence for those at the front. On that short trip Darren decided on a change of tactics: he wouldn't say a word about the new machine. Lee keenly awaited his brother's reaction when the bike was wheeled out of the workshop, and was taken aback when Darren's face reflected no emotion whatsoever. If Uncle Ken was surprised by that lack of interest he didn't show it, either: he was simply thankful that a truce of sorts was in existence.

The reaction of other competitors when they reached the craggy Kingskettle circuit was altogether more satisfying to Lee. Namura had turned up with a promotional caravan and display unit; two of their girls, in green and white outfits, were giving away advertising material and souvenirs such as bike-shaped badges and pens with tiny models of bikes floating along a motocross circuit from clip to tip. Word had got out that the rider of the first Namura to be raced at Kingskettle was Lee Parnaby, of the Skalbrooke Club. So there was a crowd of onlookers awaiting the first sighting as Ken Wragby prepared to unload.

'Hey, fantastic! And what a colour scheme!' exclaimed Nathan Pike, nowadays regarded as Lee's chief rival as Skalbrooke.

'Nobody'll miss seeing you, Lee,' Natalie Carlyle observed. She liked Lee as much as Joanne did but she'd never admit it to a soul.

Others just stared at it, almost in awe, without saying a word, and one or two asked if they could just sit in the saddle for a moment.

To Lee's relief, Darren had disappeared, taking his Kawasaki with him so that he could escape the family scene for a while. So Lee was spared his brother's usual biting, sarcastic comments. Instead, he received some very friendly remarks, even though he could detect a fair amount of envy. Nobody at all appeared really jealous of his good fortune.

'Doesn't matter what you're riding, you've still

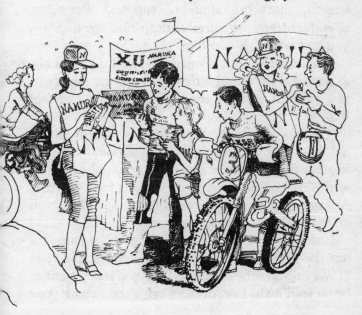

got to conquer this track,' said Stevie Stranahan, one of the welcoming committee of the Kingskettle Whistlers Club. 'I mean, it looks a lot easier than it is. I know, I'm still finding out things about it I didn't know existed – and I've ridden it a hundred times!'

'So where's the big problem, then?' Lee wanted to know. He appreciated this helpful approach; at many meetings the host riders wouldn't give visitors even a hint of a clue about the ramifications of their circuit.

'Just below the summit, on a fairly narrow stretch, short but straight,' supplied Stevie, an open-faced boy with lively, deep blue eyes. 'Show you just where, if you like.'

'Well, thanks. But if you don't mind, I always like to have a walk round a new track on my own first, just to, well, get my thoughts together,' Lee told him.

'OK, suit yourself,' replied Stevie, not at all put out by Lee's rejection of his invitation. 'Tell you another thing, though: this track used to be rubbish until they put new jumps in. Now it's a lot of fun. Anyway, I'm looking forward to racing against you on your new bike, Lee. And beating you!'

Joanne, who'd been standing beside Lee through-out the conversation, hadn't said a word. Now, as Stevie moved off, she asked: 'Do you really want to be on your own, Lee, or can I come round with you?

I mean, I need to see the track, too.'

Lee's hesitation wasn't even noticed. 'OK, so let's go now.' Suddenly it felt a terrible wrench to leave the bike and so he gave it a fond pat as if making a promise that he'd soon be back.

The hillside, with its jutting outcrops of rock on different levels, certainly was steep; as usual, on glancing for the first time at a fresh circuit, it wasn't easy to make out the lay-out. This one seemed to resemble one figure of eight inside the top loop of another, but Lee realised that wasn't entirely possible. Still, it undeniably was going to be an interesting ride . . . .

'Look,' said Joanne, pointing towards one of the most severe bends away to their right. 'There's Daz with that new mate of his. Plotting something, if I know him.'

'That's Rupert Hoyte – Rupe the Loop,' said Lee, surprised he hadn't guessed earlier who Daz's new friend must be. 'Didn't you say you'd heard him talking about speedway and how all you've got to do is go faster and faster round the loop? He can't wait to get into that. Hope he takes Daz with him. Then life'll be better all round in our motocross.'

'Daz'll be desperate to put one over on you because of your new bike, you know,' Jo warned.

Lee shrugged. 'I *do* know. He's bound to try something, like that time when he had the nerve to *boot* me out of the way during a race! But if the

Namura goes as fast as I think it will he'll never catch me round here. No one will!'

'I just might,' his cousin said rather quietly. 'I mean, I am riding your *old* bike and that isn't bad, is it? *You* did pretty well on it.'

'Well, if anybody does beat me I hope it's you,' Lee told her gallantly. 'Uncle Ken would be pretty chuffed about that whatever he says about girls riding.'

They reached the top level and soon spotted the stretch that Stevie Stranahan had called a problem. Just after an artifical jump, constructed with the help of a wooden ramp, a stream meandered across the track; it had been only partly diverted and thus some of the terrain was distinctly boggy. Really the only way to avoid it was for a rider to climb up on to a very narrow ledge that protruded from the hillside, a ledge that would take only one machine at a time from the look of it. It was protected by posts which, in turn, kept spectators at a safe distance.

'Yeah, could be tricky that one,' Lee noted. 'You'll be in a lot of trouble if you charge into that porridgey stuff. The ledge is the best bet.'

'If you say so,' murmured Joanne, thinking that trying to ride at speed along the ledge might be even more difficult, particularly if another rider was just ahead of you or someone was trying to overtake at that point.

As they made their way down to the pits where

frantic final preparations were taking place before the first race it started to rain quite heavily. On such a bleak hillside there was nowhere to shelter. Lee pulled the hood of his anorak over his head and hunched his shoulders. But Joanne seemed quite unaffected by the savagery of the downpour.

'I really don't care, I really don't care – I'm racing at last and that's all I *do* care about,' she sang.

'You won't think that if you get bogged down up there in a mud pit,' Lee declared. 'You'll need all your strength to drag a bike through that sort of stuff, you know. And it can clog up everything.'

'Might even spoil your lovely white wheels and saddle!' she grinned, refusing to be put off by any dire forecasts. 'Wouldn't it be awful if you won and nobody recognised you because you were covered in mud? Those Namura people would be choked about that!'

'They claim the tyres and saddle have been treated with some special water and mud repellent so there won't be any problem about that,' Lee retorted confidently.

Joanne remained unconvinced. 'I'll believe it when I see it.'

Even though the race would shortly be starting, the Namura was still the centre of attention and Lee had almost to push his way through the throng to reach it. Greg Shearsmith and his father, always in the forefront on the subject of new technology, were asking questions which Ken Wragby was plainly finding difficult to answer. He was looking a little harassed and appeared relieved to see his younger nephew.

'Er, I think Lee and I've got a private bit of talking to do, folks, if you don't mind,' Mr Wragby said apologetically.

'Doesn't matter how smart the bike is, it's the rider that counts,' Greg remarked as he moved away, casting a sharp glance at Lee.

'Well, you should know!' Lee whipped back with a huge grin. He believed he had little to fear from the Shearsmith Special, which had been around for a couple of seasons without winning many contests, or its pilot.

'Tell you something, Lee,' reported Uncle Ken. 'Old man Shearsmith's been trying to sell his services to the Namura people, presumably in exchange for a new bike for young Greg. But I got the impression they didn't want to know. Well, now, how d'you like the look of this circuit? The local boys think it's going to be hard for an outsider to pick up the right line straightaway.'

'Could be. The whole thing's a bit like a roller-coaster, all sharp drops and sudden bends. Oh, and this rain won't help . . . bound to make it really treacherous in places.'

'Well, you can only do your best. Look, start her up now you've got your gear on. I'll just check that everything's OK with Darren and – '

' – And don't forget about me, Dad. I'm racing, too, you know!'

'Oh, er, yes, of course. Sorry, Joanne.' Her father looked harassed again. 'Be back in a sec.'

Blue exhaust smoke was mushrooming skywards as the assembling riders began to weave patterns across the open turf in front of the start line. Lee could sense that he and his emerald green machine were still a focus of attention with spectators and fellow competitors keen to see them on the move. That was adding to the tension he always experienced during the countdown to the race itself. It wasn't that he felt nervous: it was just that he wanted the action to start. Mike Martin had arrived rather late but he dashed over for a final word: 'Best of luck, Lee. We're all rooting for you. I just know you're going to give Namura a dream start here and now.' All Lee could do was to nod his thanks. His helmet and goggles were firmly in place; his mouth was drier than it had been seconds earlier.

Joanne, somehow looking a slighter figure than usual, had been drawn away to Lee's right and almost next to Darren. It seemed strange to him that she should now be riding the bike that had been such a part of him for so many thrilling races. Normally he didn't give any thought to other riders – they were simply his rivals – but he wished he'd gone over to Joanne to wish her luck. It mattered to him very much that she should do well in her first race; and that she should emerge from it completely unscathed.

The line formed as neatly as it would ever do, the revs were reaching a crescendo, eyes were riveted to the starter. The elastic tape catapulted to one side, the roar was like thunder.

They were away!

# Five:   Racing from the Front

Almost at once, they came to the first rise, a fierce right-hander from a wide, sweeping curve that allowed no margin for manoeuvre: if you weren't in the leading group and holding the favoured line then you had to risk being bounced off the track or, more sensibly, slow down and choose another gear.

The surge from the start was all that Lee had hoped for: he was as fast away as anyone with only Stevie Stranahan on a Kawasaki in his field of vision. Another front wheel thrust forward, nearly touching his right knee, but then fell back as Lee began to lean in anticipation of the sweep to the right. Exhilarating: that was how he felt about those first seconds on the Kingskettle circuit. Up the slope he charged, veering not a centimetre from the chosen route. The higher he went the more like a tightrope it would become: a false move, a tilt one way or the other, and he could go tumbling down into oblivion. That was the joy as well as the terror of motocross.

It was at the top of the first loop that he risked a glance behind him, something he'd been told times without number by Uncle Ken and various officials never to do. 'Just keep going,' they urged. 'If you're in front that's what matters. Doesn't matter what's going on behind you. Because it *is* behind you. Something you need to know nothing about.' But he couldn't resist knowing. On this first ever ride on his new bike he needed to know how good it was, what sort of distance it had put him ahead of the rest. Well, he *convinced* himself he needed to know.

Astonishing! He was already at least five bike-lengths in front of his nearest pursuer, the local hero, Stevie Stranahan, who had the novel (and some thought rather alarming) habit of wearing a scarf while racing.

Yet, he reflected, he hadn't *seemed* to be travelling so much faster than usual at the start of a race, except during those first few vital seconds. Perhaps the truth was that everyone else was being much more cautious on this precipitous track. Just ahead of him came the first fearsome drop, after which he would turn back to face the following pack for a few metres before ascending again. That would give him a better opportunity to see who else was in a challenging position – and whether he was extending his lead.

Rupert Hoyte was the rider surprising most people, including himself. Determined to impress

everyone with his skills so that *he* could secure sponsorship for his plan to launch a junior speedway club, Rupe the Loop got off to a flier that was better than even he'd hoped for: his highly-tuned KTM provided superb initial acceleration and he himself didn't lack nerve. Prepared to throw himself into almost any situation, he was tackling these formidable gradients with brain as well as bravado. But he hadn't expected to be pushing Stevie Stranahan for second place at this stage.

Darren, who'd intended to keep close company with his new pal, was less happy: in truth, he was furious, which wasn't an abnormal state for him. As he shot from the starting-line his closest neighbour, a Kawasaki-mounted girl from the Kingskettle Club, suddenly performed an unexpected wheelie in her eagerness to achieve a flying start. In her effort to regain control of the bike she toppled to the left – and cannoned into Darren, practically knocking him over. That contact actually saved her from a premature exit from the race. For, bouncing off her neighbour, her bike resumed an upright position and she was able to regain control and re-enter the frantic charge for the awesome first ascent. She was virtually oblivious to what had really happened to her at the start and certainly had no idea she'd just about knocked a fellow competitor out of the contest.

Spitting imprecations in all directions, Daz even had to cope with re-starting his engine because it cut out during the collision. Although not always so perceptive he had recognised that the culprit was a girl. So, in customary fashion, he was able to blame his brother for his trouble: Lee was one of those nutters (Daz's word) who encouraged females to participate in motocross and therefore cause the sort of mayhem of which Darren himself had just been such a hapless victim. So that was another reason to get even with his Lee-tle brother as he'd recently taken to calling him, a pun that he thought was hysterically funny. The only irritation was that Lee himself wasn't reacting to it. But Daz wasn't one to change his target or his method of trying to hit it: and his target now was the race leader who was going to be removed from that position.

Joanne, who could usually guess what was in Darren's mind, was adopting a careful approach to her first race. She'd never have admitted it to Lee, but the severity of the circuit was daunting. Naturally, she wanted to do well and finish her first race in a good position: but the vital thing was simply *to finish*. If, for any reason at all, she failed to complete the course her Dad might well begin to wonder whether he'd done the right thing in allowing her to race. So she'd be on trial not just for a couple of races but very likely for weeks. Another mistake and the Honda would probably be handed to Darren. That was something to be avoided at all costs. So she was determined to do as well as she could but attempt nothing spectacular however tempting a chance might be. When she entered the first switch-back sequence she saw that Lee was leading the field and she was thrilled for him. He'd been marvellous about the Honda and supporting her claim: so anything she could do for him she would, without hesitation.

Just ahead of her was Greg Shearsmith. Like Darren, he wasn't happy about the turn of events. These days the famed Shearsmith Special seemed to have lost its zip – or perhaps his father had simply lost his touch. In the past he'd always competed on equal terms, or better, with the other Skalbrooke riders; nowadays he knew he was in an inferior position. Greg believed he was at least as good a competitor as Lee Parnaby. Yet there was Lee on the green and white superbike, not just leading but *pulling away* from everybody else. Greg was determined to get a bike just like that, even if it meant doing something quite desperate. Meanwhile, he was an keen as ever to cut down the riders in front of him, one of whom, he spotted, was Rupe Hoyte who'd recently had the effrontery to tell Greg he was 'just a failed show-off on a cheap, home-made black bike!' Well, Greg was going to make Loopy Rupy eat those foul words.

Up in front, Lee was thinking only about his own performance. By now he was well beyond the squelchy stretch just under the summit and there'd been a good cheer from spectators as he rose over the jump and landed safely. Although he didn't catch sight of him Mike Martin had stationed himself at that point. Watching keenly every aspect of Lee's control of the bike he was well satisfied. Namura had chosen well, he told himself (by which he meant that he himself had chosen well). Boy and bike appeared to have a natural affinity and success on their first outing would be excellent publicity. Kingskettle didn't provide the ultimate test of motocross skills (whatever riders like Stevie Stranaham and Nathan Pike thought), but it still provided a guide to what a biker like Lee might accomplish; the real criterion was the circuit at Taplow Castle which would really sort out the second-raters the following week. Mike was looking forward to the action there.

As he neared the end of the first circuit Lee again risked a glance to see what was happening behind him. If anything, Stevie had dropped back still further and was being chivvied along by Rupert, now giving everything he'd got to try and wrest second spot; and when it was his Rupe would be flat out for the lead. Lee thought he could just make out Joanne in the middle of the main pack but of Daz there was no sign. That was worrying. His brother must surely be in some sort of trouble; and that would make him more dangerous than ever as a rival. Could he, though, have had a spill and be out of contention altogether?

Lee sensed that Rupert was simply showing off: he would want to let everyone see that you didn't need a brand new superbike to be a super rider. So the Namura was definitely affecting him. Was it causing other riders to suspect they were beaten already, that they had no hope of overtaking what some spectators were now calling The Green Machine?

To polite applause from some and a great cheer from his uncle, who also held his arms wide to indicate that he was well in front, Lee completed the first lap in what was almost record time for the Kingskettle track. He'd never been so far in front at this stage of any previous motocross and it was a wonderful feeling. If he kept going at this rate he might even start lapping the stragglers. Perhaps Darren would be among them! That thought was so refreshing, Lee edged on to a new line that would reduce his own lap time still further if he could adhere to it all the way round.

The first major calamity occurred only seconds later. Two riders unwilling to give a centimetre's advantage to the other went for the same narrow angle on a fairly easy left-hander: and collided heavily. Both riders fell away from their bikes just as Lee came upon the scene.

It wasn't hard to avoid one of them – but practically impossible to miss both because their bikes, one an ancient Suzuki, were entangled with each other in between them. Instantaneously, he decided to get up on the bank, little more than a fragile ridge on the left. Dexterously he flicked through the gears, braced himself fleetingly with his right leg, braked, slithered back down the bank on to the track, accelerated again. He had lost none of his momentum.

Lee was thrilled. He'd passed his first real test in flawless fashion. What's more, the Namura had responded perfectly. Braking and acceleration and balance were all that the manufacturers claimed them to be. At that moment he had no doubt at all that he was going to win on his first ride on The Green Machine. It really wouldn't matter what Stevie and Rupert and Nathan and the rest of them did in the next few laps.

Darren, though, had other ideas. His progress since that unhappy start hadn't been good. Twice he'd been forced to brake heavily to avoid disaster on a couple of the turns while the quagmire immediately after the highest jump had nearly claimed him for its own. Assistance had been needed from spectators to push him clear when he strayed from his chosen line and his rear wheel ceased to revolve momentarily. Of course, he mentally rehearsed the perfect excuse to present to Uncle Ken: 'This machine's past it. Just can't cope with the wet. Seizes up. I'll have to a have a new one.' Today wasn't going to be his day; but Daz was going to make sure that tomorrow things would be much better. Meanwhile, he could see that Lee was going to cruise to victory. Unless he, Darren, could stop him. . . .

The leader was beginning to pick off the hopeless ones, threading his way through the minefield of lost causes, aware that Stevie's battle was with Nathan to hold on to second place, not challenge for supremacy. Lee really was enjoying himself.

Even the rain, still falling, though much less

heavily, wasn't really bothering him. There was, though, some suction as he ploughed through the area fed by the partly-diverted stream and it occurred to him that next time round he ought to take a different line. That might cost him a second or two but he could afford it with the sort of lead he was holding at present.

By now several competitors were out of the race, victims of their own impatience or someone else's recklessness. Even Stevie nearly came to grief after being overtaken by Nathan: he resented the relegation so much that he flung caution aside, went in pursuit on a downhill stretch, failed to brake in time on a corner and slithered horribly into the bank. Luckily for him, he escaped any injury and the bike was undamaged. But now he was in fourth place because Natalie Carlyle, riding at her most brilliant, cruised past while Stevie was re-mounting.

Not all of Ken Wragby's attention was concentrated on his nephews. At first he'd shown little enough interest in how Joanne was getting on. But Natalie's performance had reminded him that he ought to be watching his own daughter. After all, Joanne was not letting the family down. As she ticked off the laps her confidence was building up; neither race nor circuit were as difficult as she'd feared before setting out on her first motocross. By now she'd even passed a few rivals and although she had no real hope of finishing in the first half-dozen she was keen to get a high placing.

'Come on, girl, come on!' her dad yelled as she swept past him again. She couldn't hear what he was saying but his gestures plainly indicated support. So that cheered her, too. Her sights now were set on catching Darren because, much to her surprise, he wasn't far ahead of her. Indeed, he almost seemed to be coming back towards her, making her wonder whether he was having bike trouble.

He wasn't. The slowing down was deliberate, all part of his grand design . . . the plan that would give Lee-tle brother something to think about. As one of his teachers had grudgingly remarked, Darren had a pocket calculator in place of a brain. What he was calculating now, as he approached the high jump ahead of the soggy stretch, was the precise moment to strike. On the previous couple of bends he'd seen that Lee was on the point of overtaking him (well that, of course, as Daz told himself, was because he was *permitting* it). Lee would want to accomplish that with a flourish, Darren decided. So just let him try it . . . .

Lee was relishing the prospect. Darren seemed to have been riding an erratic race, now powering ahead, now braking and looking to be in trouble, perhaps with mechanical trouble. But he didn't pull off the track. Scooting past him on the top stretch wouldn't be easy but it might be very satisfying if poor old Daz caught the edge of the swamp!

Daz, idling no longer, approaches the ramp, Lee right on his tail. Lee thinks he'd love to overtake in mid-air but knows that's just not possible. Still, immediately afterwards it will be. They touch down simultaneously. Daz, with perfect timing, leans to the left, swerving across the face of the quagmire. Lee's too close to brake: he'd smash into his brother amidships if he did. So he must go left, too. With no loss of pace.

With the sort of skill he so rarely shows, Daz succeeds in carrying Lee out. Then, just as the bank comes up, he swerves right again, finding the margin of the swamp and keeping to it. He'll get through but no one else could have managed it in cold blood. Judgment is as accurate as timing.

Lee rears up on the bank, no other option open to him. Sees the post ahead of him but can't avoid it; just manages to miss hitting it head-on. It's his left arm that crunches into it. Pain doesn't really strike through yet because all his nerves and senses are battling for survival. To keep upright, to stay in the race. To get back on the track.

Which, moments later, he succeeds in doing, still at racing speed, still in front, still set on winning with style in a course record time. The wooden post is knocked askew by the impact with the rider but it's still in position, still firmly embedded in the

ground. It came off a little better than its opponent.

Daz remains in front of his brother for hardly more than fifty metres. His teeth grind, his eyes glower, as Lee, unimpeded after all, speeds past. Daz, his best trick played, has lost, is lapped and left behind.

It took Lee almost half a lap to come to terms with what had happened; so for that distance he was riding more or less instinctively. Daz had very nearly put him out of the race for good. His luck was both in and out: it was in that he'd managed to scale the bank – and out because he'd struck the post.

He'd managed to navigate the ridge because he'd done it before and he could put that down to good planning.

Daz: he felt like murdering him! He was well aware that his elder brother was capable of trying anything but this latest episode was something he hadn't expected. And that was why Darren had almost succeeded in outwitting him. He'd struck when Lee was feeling smug and quite pleased with himself. Well, at least he'd failed in his objective. Lee was still in the race, still in front, still confident of winning. But the pain in his forearm was now getting worse.

He gritted his teeth and kept going. There was nothing else to do. With only a couple of laps to go he would make it. Nathan, he saw, was in second place and had closed on him a fraction: but only a fraction. Natalie was duelling with Stevie for third place but what Joanne's position was he had no idea. Just before Darren carried out his ambush Lee had been thinking that he missed Joanne's track-side signals telling him how he stood in the context of the race. It hadn't occurred to Uncle Ken to take over that role.

The chequered flag came up for Lee. If his arm hadn't been hurting so much he might have done a celebratory wheelie. As it was, he was thankful he could now switch off. He managed a wave to acknowledge the applause from the spectators but that was all.

'You all right, Lee?' his uncle asked anxiously when he reached the paddock and pulled his helmet off. 'You look a bit white.'

'It's my arm,' Lee explained. 'I bashed it against a post up there when Daz tried to force me out of the race. Ouch! That really hurts!'

His uncle was making a preliminary examination but it was obvious that Lee would have to take his jacket off first. Other people coming over to congratulate the Skalbrooke rider on his success paused to see the extent of the injury. Mike Martin was among them and his instant smile was vanishing.

'Oh now, that doesn't look good at all,' Ken Wragby exclaimed when he'd succeeded in removing the jacket and, with equal difficulty, folding back Lee's shirt sleeve. 'What's it feel like?'

'Terrible,' Lee admitted. 'Don't think I'll be able to ride again today.'

# Six: Victory on Ice!

Mike Martin's frown deepened as he stepped forward for a closer lok at the injured arm. Already the swelling was obvious and the bruising beginning to appear. There was even a smear of blood though where that had come from it wasn't easy to tell until Ken Wragby spotted a broken shirt button that had pierced the skin.

'You must have given that post a heck of a wallop,' one of the officials murmured. 'I'm not surprised you're in pain. I think we ought to get one of the first aid people and see if there's worse damage under the skin. Could be a –'

'Can you grip all right?' Mr Martin cut in, speaking to Lee. 'Try flexing your fingers.'

Lee did so, and winced. The pain wasn't easing at all. Perhaps he had fractured the bone, which he guessed was what the official was hinting at. In fact, he was beginning to feel a little faint and he wished all these people would stop crowding round him.

'It's not as bad as it looks,' Martin announced very positively. 'What we need is some ice. That'll get the swelling down and improve things no end. You've got at least an hour before your next race and things'll look different then.'

Uncle Ken raised an eyebrow. 'The boy's in pain, Mike. He's not going racing again in that state. It's not on. You've – '

Martin moved across to take Mr Wragby by the arm. 'He's *got* to race,' he said in a low, fierce tone. 'It's in the contract you read and signed. He's here to ride for Namura. A little sprain like that isn't going to stop him – or us.'

Ken Wragby glanced anxiously at his nephew. He wasn't sure just what he'd signed. But this wasn't the time to get involved in contractual discussions with anyone. 'What do you think, Lee?'

Lee was just wishing that someone would do something positive to help him; instead everyone was just jabbering away as if he were simply an object of scientific interest. After achieving his first ever all-the-way success he was keen to race again to prove that it was no fluke; but if he couldn't grip the machine properly because of the pain then it was pointless to try. Worse, a failure might suggest that he had been lucky the first time round.

But, before he could answer Uncle Ken's question, Daz and Joanne arrived. When she saw the look on Lee's face she swallowed her jubilation at finishing ninth and asked what on earth had happened.

'Ask him, he did it, the rat,' replied Lee, nodding at his brother. For once, no one complained about his abusive language.

Darren assumed one of his most-practised expressions: a mixture of amazement and put-upon innocence. 'Don't know what you mean. I just had to swerve to miss some deep mud. Didn't know you were that close. Anyway, what've you done to yourself?'

'Can't you see how bad his arm is, Darren?' his uncle said sharply. 'A marker post did that to him.'

Predictably, there was no sympathy from Daz. 'Well, he should have avoided that post. He's always going on about how good a rider he is. So he should prove it by avoiding obstacles, not hitting 'em. That's – '

'I did,' Lee said through clenched teeth. 'That's how I won the race, by going *faster* round everything than anybody else, including *you*. You must've finished nearly last. And that's just where you deserve to be. You – '

'Look, this is no time for family feuds,' interrupted Mike Martin, asserting his authority. 'Let's get that ice I was talking about. We'll have some in our fridge in the promotions van. But we'll need more than that. Joanne, do you think you could round some up from somewhere? And anyone else who's not doing anything for a minute.'

Joanne scuttled away immediately. Darren mooched away, whether to look for ice or to find his friend Rupe he didn't say. One or two riders came up, ostensibly to offer Lee congratulations but in some cases to scrutinise his injury. Crashes of one sort or another were such a regular occurrence in motocross that practically everybody had suffered damage; broken legs and cracked collar-bones topped the list, in spite of all the protective clothing, and fingers were twisted and sprained frequently. A swollen arm wasn't particularly interesting and so those of a morbid nature soon drifted away in search of genuine excitement to fill the gap before the next race.

'Come on, let's get you sitting down and comfortable, Lee,' said Mike Martin in a kinder tone. 'We'll use our van. Then you can tell me about the race. It was great to see you win. You looked fantastic out there on the Green Machine! This result will be a big boost for our sales people, I can tell you.'

Lee didn't really feel in the mood to analyse the race he'd just ridden in but it was only fair to Namura to tell them what he could. Mike Martin asked a lot of pertinent questions and made copious notes until Joanne interrupted them. In addition to

81

scrounging loose ice from various acquaintances she'd also got hold of a plastic-coated ice pack of the kind used in travelling freezer bags: and that was promptly placed on Lee's forearm with a towel wrapped around it.

'So, how's that feel?' Uncle Ken asked when he came in moments later. 'You've got a bit more colour in your cheeks since I last saw you!'

Lee, still gasping with the coldness of the contact, admitted that perhaps there was a tiny improvement. What he meant was that it was a different kind of pain since the ice pack had been applied.

'Good, good,' rejoiced Martin. 'Keep on flexing your fingers, Lee. Don't want them to seize up!'

For the next few minutes money was what he and Ken Wragby talked about, almost as if Lee wasn't present. Mike disclosed that he was 'more than hopeful' of landing some advertising contracts for various 'spots' on the green-and-white Namura riding gear that Lee was now wearing as part of the deal with the motorcycle company. Inevitably, one of them was with an oil company, who'd probably choose the band across the chest. The area on the helmet above the eyes was under discussion with the manufacturers of a new brand of toothpaste.

'Good at cleaning your teeth, are you, son – er, Lee?' Mike suddenly inquired.

Lee, who hadn't been listening, was startled. 'Well, er, sort of but not every day. I mean what – '

'Oh, don't worry. I don't suppose these people will send a representative to examine your teeth before every race! But you could get some extra pocket money out of this, Lee.'

'Good.' Lee was beginning to experience a shut-in feeling. Too many people kept talking over him. 'Look, I need to go to the loo. Excuse me.'

Mike wouldn't let him go as easily as that. 'So how's the arm feeling now?'

Lee shrugged. 'Can't tell yet.'

'Well, keep flexing the fingers. We want you racing again in less than half-an-hour. One win isn't nearly as good as two, you know.'

Lee knew that. As he made his way across the paddock he was thinking that they didn't seem to realise that he was just as keen to win as they were. There were always those riders who declared that any single victory by a rival was bound to be a fluke. In his case, they'd say that it was the bike that won simply because it was a supercharged new model that couldn't fail whoever rode it. He knew that would be Daz's view – if Daz failed to get a Namura for himself. So Lee realised that it was important for several reasons, including his own self-esteem, for him to ride again as soon as possible – and win again.

'How're you feeling now, Lee?' Joanne asked anxiously as he emerged from the rustic toilet that stood like a sentry box, surrounded by canvas, at a corner of the field.

'I think it's a bit better, actually,' he told her, wiggling his fingers quite vigorously. 'Mike Martin's ice trick seems to be working. I mean, there's still *some* pain but I suppose I can cope with that.'

'Heroes can cope with anything!' she grinned. For once he wasn't sure whether she was mocking him or not. But she knew what he was thinking. 'No, I mean it, Lee. I mean, if you win you must be a hero, if you fail you're, well, useless. And you also survived Darren's attack. So what are you going to do about the dastardly Daz? I heard that word the other day and I think it just suits him.'

'Nothing, I suppose. He didn't put me out of the race, which he was trying to do; and he finished at the back of the field. So that proves just how useless he is. I don't have to do anything else, Jo.'

She wasn't convinced that was the right course. 'He may have a go at you again. And then – '

'Not here, he won't. Officials will be watching him after what he did up at the swamp. He wouldn't get away with it a second time.'

'Hope you're right, and I hope you win again – if I don't!' she said as they reached the Namura van. There a St John Ambulance Brigade girl was waiting to take a professional look at his injury which, she decided, wasn't serious. His arm was given a spray treatment and then strapped up; and Lee was declared fit to ride in the next race. Mr Martin, naturally, was wreathed in smiles again. The Green

Machine was going to be seen in action again, after all.

'Look, just take care of yourself,' Uncle Ken told his younger nephew before he joined the starting line. 'If you feel woozy or anything like that just pull out. Nobody'll think any the worse of you. Remember, your health comes first. Oh, and I've warned Darren that if he tries any more of his funny tricks I'll take his bike away from him – if the Club secretary doesn't ban him first.'

Before they switched all their attention to the starter, awaiting his signal for another hectic launching, Lee and Joanne wished each other good luck. Lee felt guilty. He realised he'd forgotten to compliment his cousin on her own excellent performance in her first race. But he'd had a lot of other matters on his mind. . . .

In fact, neither of them did as well second time round the Kingskettle circuit. Lee failed to get the flying start he'd hoped for and then was severely impeded at the foot of the first steep climb when two riders came off and one slithered right across his path. Although the rain had ceased the surface was distinctly greasy and so lost ground was even harder to make up. This time Stevie Stranahan arrowed into the lead which he was still increasing at the end of the first lap. Natalie Carlyle, eager to be the second visiting winner, was in hot pursuit with Nathan Pike a bike-length behind in third place.

Lee and Joanne were in the middle of the field and virtually in tandem but Darren was an early casualty when he completely misjudged the sharpness of an S-bend and fell of his bike, winding himself quite severely (in his own opinion).

Lee could not make up all the deficit, hard as he tried; his arm was troubling him only a little and that was something he couldn't use as an excuse for failure. In truth, Stevie, riding in excellent form, controlled the race very well. He didn't expect to be beaten on his own track and defeat in the first event added another edge to his ambition to stay at the top. Natalie held off the rest of the competition to be second and Lee felt his fifth place was really quite respectable.

Mike Martin was inclined to agree when he and the Wragby and Parnaby families got together afterwards by the Namura van.

'You did really well, son – sorry, *Lee* – especially after your battle with the marker post. Namura can be proud of you – and I hope you're proud of the Namura product.'

'Oh, sure. Thanks. Yeah, I think it's a great bike and I'm really looking forward to the next race. I – '

'Good, good, *good*! Because that's the big one, the one where we're really flying the flag and hoping to pull in the publicity and sell a lot of bikes. Next weekend at Taplow Castle's going to be one of the highlights of the whole season. That's why we're putting you up at the Castle itself overnight.' He paused to let everyone start to express their surprise with widening eyes, raised eyebrows and dropped jaws. 'Yeah, that's how special it is, folks. Super place, the Castle, just like a four-star country hotel in its own grounds. Oh, and the food's supposed to be terrific, too.'

'Hey, I hope I'm getting an invite to this place, too,' Darren said aggressively. 'I mean, I'm part of this family and where he goes, I go. I should be chosen *first* because I'm the elder.'

'Well . . . ' said Mike Martin, doubtfully, casting a 'help-me' look at Uncle Ken.

'Look, when Lee crashes again I'll be the one to take his place because I'm the real class rider in the family,' Darren went on, desperate to reinforce his claim.

'But you crashed out of the race here!' Lee pointed out.

'No, I didn't. Just hit a skiddy patch, that's all. And the bike wasn't right after that. If I had a Namura like you I'd win everything in sight!'

'You're just a vulture, waiting for Lee to hurt himself,' Joanne said scathingly.

'No, I'm a realist,' Darren retorted with an unexpected smile.

Joanne wasn't finished with: she wasn't going to be upstaged by Darren. 'Listen, if anything does go wrong for Lee then *I* should be the replacement.

I've had two rides today and finished in a high place both times. *And* I've already ridden a Namura and shown I can handle it. Mr Barrow, the boss, said I was really good on it, didn't he, Mr Martin?'

'Er, yes, I think he said something like that,' agreed Mike, now with more worries.

Ken Wragby decided it was time he intervened. 'This isn't the time or the place for a family squabble. Let's wait until we get home before we start sorting out what's going to happen next week-end. Lee – '

But Lee had his own view on what would happen. 'Nothing's going to go wrong for me,' he said very positively. 'I'll be riding the Namura and I'll be the winner.'

'Don't count on it, Lee-tle,' Darren murmured. But he said it too softly for anyone to hear.

# Seven:  Shooting-the-stairs

'D'you know,' said Joanne, leaning back luxuriously in her upholstered dining chair, 'I could live like this for the rest of my life. Great food, waited on hand and foot, a bedroom with its own bathroom! I mean, who could want anything else?'

'I agree,' responded Natalie, fiddling with a fastening behind her neck for her long blonde hair. She watched a young trainee waitress carrying a huge metal tray of empty dishes to the serving hatch at the far end of the flagged dining area. 'What was the name of that chicken dish again? Chaser, or something? Fantastic!'

'*Chasseur*,' supplied Joanne who was becoming increasingly interested in the subject of cooking. 'I think it means it's specially for the hunter. French, *je pense*.'

'Well, *I* think I'm going to do a bit more hunting around this place. Judging by the view of the courtyard from our bedroom we haven't seen even *half* of Taplow Castle yet.' Natalie had a natural curiosity about almost everything and as they'd been told they had the rest of the evening to themselves she wasn't going to miss a chance to explore a real castle that might contain dungeons or even a ghost. 'Any of you boys want to come and look round this place with us? I mean, you are coming with me, Joanne?'

'You must be joking!' Nathan said, frowning at such a ludicrous suggestion. 'Didn't you hear about the video they're putting on for us in the library? Last year's 500cc World Championship, that's all! Best motocross you'll ever see in your life. You can't miss that, Tally.'

'Oh yes I can,' replied his near-namesake. 'Anyway, you might see something even better tomorrow when I – oh, and Joanne – get going on the Castle circuit.'

'Get lost!' remarked Lee. But he wasn't being unfriendly and he smiled as he said it.

'You know, I like Lee, he's definitely got a sense of humour,' said Natalie as they sauntered out of the dining room, a remark which made Joanne'e eyebrows rise. 'But his brother, that Darren, can't *stand* him at any price. He's so, *arrogant*. Yet what's he ever done? I mean, how did *he* get on the invitation list?'

'Blackmail, really. You know my dad looks after his and Lee's bikes? Well, when Lee got invited because of Namura, Darren just kicked up a terrific fuss, saying he was the elder and that sort of thing. Everything he could think of, including, would you believe, that he should be the official stand-in if Lee was injured! Well Dad believes in treating them the same so he just had to give in and wangle an invite for the dastardly Daz.'

Natalie shook her head at such behaviour. 'Well, at least he'll be out of his class from what I hear about the other people who'll be riding here tomorrow. Like this guy Finn Beanland, the Flying Finn somebody said they call him. And Stevie the Scarf – you know, Stevie Stranahan from Kingskettle. Then there's this girl I was warned about: Adrienne Tuff. How about that for a name? Hope she doesn't live up to it in a bad sort of way!'

Instinctively they turned off the corridor they were exploring when they discovered it led directly to the kitchens and instead decided to investigate a narrow staircase that looked interesting.

'But I could be out of my depth, too,' Joanne pointed out. 'I've hardly done any racing and I certainly haven't won anything. I only got invited becuase of my dad and the Namura people. They said it was a reward because they're using my photo in publicity shots for the new bike.'

'No, you deserve to be here, Jo. You've got style. Anybody seeing you ride can tell that. All you need is a bit more experience and maybe a bit of a confidence booster. Hey, where do you think these stairs lead to? I bet they were for the servants to get up to their attic rooms. Probably right up in those turrets. Can't wait to see what it's like up there!'

They emerged, through a curiously arched door-way, onto a short corridor that then opened out into a gallery that overlooked the main hall.

'Hey, what a height!' Joanne exclaimed. 'You could hang-glide to the ground floor from up here. Oh, and look at those pictures down there, the ones on the wall by the main staircase. Colossal! I mean, they'd cover – just one of them – the entire wall of our lounge at home.'

'You know, I love looking at old portraits, imagining what the people were like, what sort of friends and families they had, their secret *passions*! Great fun,' Natalie enthused. 'Come on, let's have a look at those.'

The main staircase started one level below them and was as broad as it was grand, turning three times at right angles before reaching ground level. The girls had to find another flight of ordinary steps at the other end of the gallery in order to reach the head of the grand staircase where the first of the huge oil paintings was hanging by metal chains.

Joanne stared down at the tiled hall, illuminated by no fewer than three chandeliers, and wondered what it would be like to descend that staircase, wearing a ball gown, her hand resting lightly on the arm of the handsomest young man, as the sounds of a waltz drifted upwards from the ballroom. Would, that night, her escort propose to her and would she – '

'Tell you what,' Natalie cut in to Joanne's dreams destructively, 'this staircase would make a great downhill section for a motocross! Can you just imagine sweeping round these turns, touching the brake here, touch more there, then really letting your Honda rev off along that corridor?'

'Not really,' replied Joanne, not wanting to exchange one fantasy for another just yet. 'Bikes would just ruin the woodwork, especially if anybody bounced into the banisters. Except those banisters are so solid you'd probably crack your head open. Must have used whole oak trees for this lot.'

'Well, then, a cresta run,' Natalie continued, unwilling to suppress her imagination. 'Those winter sports toboggans you see on TV shooting down an ice channel, rocking from side to side. Terrific speed. At our house I once got a tray and sat on that and shot down our stairs. And – and – '

She stopped as if struck by lightning. Her eyes appeared glazed for a moment and Joanne was worried. 'Listen, I've just had a great, *great* idea!' she exclaimed, her eyes lighting up again. 'We could have a race, a race down these stairs on those huge trays they served our dinner on! It'd be a fantastic experience. Bet the boys would love it. What d'you think, Jo?'

Joanne was momentarily speechless. It seemed a crazy idea but she began to get caught up in Natalie's excitement. 'But we'd never get away with it, Tally. They wouldn't let us have the trays for something like that. And even if we pinched them when they weren't looking they'd hear all the noise and come and – '

'No, no, it'd work! We've just got to wait until the staff go off duty. You know they told us they don't live here in the main house. So we'll have the place practically to ourselves. Nobody'll hear us and we won't do any damage. That's got to be Number One rule.'

Joanne was remembering something else all the visiting riders had been told: that they were being trusted to behave 'sensibly and with consideration for others, including the castle itself, at all times.' That's why they weren't under supervision every hour of their stay. Both the manager of the Taplow Castle leisure complex and the housekeeper slept on the premises but they had their own self-contained flats and weren't to be disturbed except in an emergency. There were phones in several of the bedrooms and they connected with the manager's flat. So the only adults who were around were two of the riders' parents and they'd been given a room at the end of a corridor on the second floor.

'Come on, Jo, you're not scared, are you?' asked Natalie, misinterpreting her friend's hesitation. 'I don't want to race against the boys just on my own, you know. I want to show 'em that we girls are better than them. Remember, I've also had some practice at shooting the stairs – well, one race with myself, anyway!'

Joanne grimaced. 'Look, I don't mind having a go just with you. But if we get the boys involved, well, they'll make a din and get all carried away and – and things'll go wrong, I know it.'

'No they won't! I swear it,' Natalie insisted. 'Come on, be a sport, Jo. We'll never have a chance like this again. These stairs are just right, not too steep, not too shallow, plenty of width, perfect really. *And* those trays are the best I've ever seen.'

Without another glance at the portraits she'd been so eager to study only minutes earlier Natalie sped away across the hall to the passageway that led to the library where the rest of the motocrossers invited to the Taplow Castle Special Event were so engrossed in the video they were watching they scarcely looked up when the girls arrived and sank into easy chairs.

For a while Natalie, too, watched in silence. Then, still restless, she leaned across to Joanne: 'Just going to the kitchen to check up on the trays.

This film'll finish in a few minutes. Don't let the boys start on anything else until I get back. OK?'

'OK,' Joanne agreed without enthusiasm.

In fact, Natalie timed her return perfectly. Moments after the film ended and while everyone was still animatedly discussing it she flung open the door and posed on the threshold, holding a rectangular silver and red tray by her fingertips as if displaying a painting at an auction. Just by standing there she gained attention.

'Right, then,' she called out. 'Who can tell me what this is?'

For a moment no one said a word because they all thought the answer was too obvious to be worth giving. Then, with a rather sly grin spreading across his face, Darren suggested: 'It's for carrying off the trophies I'm going to win tomorrow!'

That was too dreadful to be worth even a look of disgust from Natalie. 'Anyone got an *intelligent* idea?' she persisted.

'You bang on it with a gong to tell everyone the next meal's ready!' offered Nathan, which drew a couple of laughs.

Natalie decided she was wasting her time. 'Right, I'll tell you as you're all too dim to work it out. This is an indoor motocross machine. It's what you ride down the stairs on in a race. OK?'

This time the momentary silence seemed to contain elements of admiration. Then there was a

babble of noise. 'Hey, great thinking!' – 'When can we try it out?' – 'Which stairs are we going to use?' – 'Bags I have the first go!'

Natalie called for silence again and explained that no one would be racing anywhere if they kept up that racket. Then she told them exactly what she had in mind.

'Come on, I want to see this staircase, see how fast I can go,' Daz dcelared the moment she paused for breath and he thought she'd finished. Predictably, he was certain he'd be the champion at this new version of his favourite sport. He was about to brush past her when she lifted the tray again and held him back by the simple expedient of pushing it into his chest.

'Hang on, Daz, I've got a job for you,' she told him. 'You've got to go to the kitchens and find another couple of trays – I know they've got more than one because I remember the ones the waitresses were carrying. And Nat, I want you to check upstairs and see if anyone's about who might hear us. Lee and Greg, could you please go and round up all the helmets and riding gear – oh and perhaps you could help, too, Adrian, to save time. Rupert, your job's to check on the front door of the Castle, see nobody's going to come and interrupt us. Now nobody *argue*. It's my idea and I'm in charge and if you don't like it you won't race. OK?'

Joanne was a little surprised that everyone did as

he was told without arguing; but then Natalie not only had an air of authority when she needed one, she had a physical strength that equalled that of almost any of the boys as she'd proved on a couple of occasions when they'd tried to mix it with her on the track. It hadn't escaped Joanne, either, that she'd cleverly kept Daz and his pal Rupert Hoyte apart when delegating the various tasks.

'I've got a job for you, too, Jo,' Natalie said to Joanne's astonishment. 'Get a bit of paper and write down everyone's name on it. You know, as if we were having a raffle. We're having a draw instead! A draw to decide who races against whom in the GSM.'

'The what?'

'The Grand Staircase Motocross,' Natalie told her with a wide grin. 'Sounds great, doesn't it? I think we can only race one against one, you see, because of the width of the stairs. So we'll have to have a knock-out competition. Still, that makes it more fun, doesn't it?'

Nobody disagreed with that, either, when everyone was assembled again. If anything, the prospect of taking part in a knock-out event was even more enticing. With due ceremony, the folded strips of paper were dropped into a helmet and given a good shake. Conveniently, there were eight riders present and so, as Darren smugly pointed out, he was already in the quarter-finals.

'We all are, you nut!' Natalie told him with a smile. 'And we'll have another draw for the semi-finals because that's only fair. Oh yes, and one special privilege for me because I thought up this idea: I get to go first whoever I'm drawn against. OK?'

Again, no one disputed that. The only thing that seemed to matter now was the draw, to be made by Natalie herself and Joanne: and quite amazingly, her own name was the first she drew out: Natalie v. Nathan. Followed by Darren v. Rupert (which caused them both to looked anguished), Lee v. Greg Shearsmith and, finally Joanne v. Adrian Linthwaite, the only rider to be invited from the Linkland Motocross Club.

'Right, let's go and have some practice,' Darren called, rushing for the first palce in the queue, as he imagined it.

'No practising, there's no time for that – and it would only make it more risky because we'd make a lot more noise,' Natalie insisted.

'But that's not fair, Tally!' Rupe protested.

'Hard cheese,' she answered crisply. 'Life's like that, Rupe. Anyway, if you're as good as you think you are you don't need to practise to beat your old mate.'

'Look, you can't fix everything,' Daz started to say when Natalie cut him off.

'I can because nobody but you is arguing against anything I say. If you don't want to follow the rules, just push off. Now, Adrian: you check the front door now because you're going last. Whoever's knocked out early on can take your place when you ride.'

When they all stood at the foot of the grand staircase for the first time and stared up at the point where the races would begin there were several gasps as they realised what they were letting themselves in for; the stairs themselves were fairly shallow but that would only encourage a rapid descent. The two right-angled turns, one to the left, one to the right, were formidable obstacles at any speed. Even Natalie looked a trifle paler as she glanced upwards. But her nerve held and she started to put on knee-pads and shoulder-protectors.

'Don't bother with all that gear – you're just wasting time,' said Daz, impatient as always.

'Anybody who rides down these stairs on a toboggan without some padding is just asking for trouble,' she retorted. 'If you hit one of those wooden posts you'll wish you'd put a duvet on! It won't be like a soft landing on one of our circuits after the rain. And you'll probably roll all the way to the bottom as well, breaking a few more bones on the way.'

'So maybe we should get some cushions or a

couple of rugs or something to soften the landing,' suggested Joanne, thinking it was time she made a contribution.

'Good idea, try the library or the lounge – the drawing-room, I think it's called,' agreed Natalie. 'OK, Nathan, time for our helter-skelter.'

Nathan, too, had put on some sensible clothing but he was wondering whether he was foolish to take part in a game like this. If he did have a bad crash it might put him out of tomorrow's races – and he desperately wanted to win one of them to improve his overall ranking in the sport.

Natalie had chosen the smaller of the trays that were being used because she felt it would be easier to control; it also had a slightly higher rim and that might be an advantage for steering purposes. This was going to be a much tougher trip than the one she'd taken at home. She licked her lips and glanced sideways at Nathan. He looked even more worried than she felt, she decided.

'Come on, you two, get going! We want our turn, you know,' Rupe yelled.

Joanne was to be starter. The riders would signal when they were ready, she would sing out, 'One, two, GO!' And away they went, no further hesitation at all, side by side for the first few steps before Natalie edged ahead. She'd got her balance right while Nathan, uneasy and uncomfortable, was striving to settle into a position of control.

The others stared, totally transfixed, as Natalie slid into the first turn and very cleverly flicked round it by holding on to a corner post for a split-second; that set up a good line for the second turn even though it meant that she was now cutting across her rival's path.

That no longer mattered. Nathan, still unsure of everything he was trying to do, simply failed to take the first corner. With a rising 'oooo-OOOH!' he slammed into the panelled wall before falling sideways off his tray. To his own great surprise, he hadn't hurt himself at all.

Sticking like superglue to her tray and her plan, Natalie skimmed round the second bend and finally ploughed triumphantly into a bed of cushions. She rolled to her feet and held her arms aloft in a joyous salute to her own achievement. It had been an exhilarating experience – and, of course, she'd won her race!

'Hey, you were great – fantastic – how did it feel, Tally?' they greeted her. No one took any notice of Nathan; but then, they rarely did sympathise with a fallen rider on a motocross circuit. Coming off was the risk they knew all about and expected would happen to them at some stage. In any case, Nathan hadn't suffered.

Already Daz, having grabbed Natalie's winning tray, and Rupert were bounding up the stairs, their rivalry now as great as their recent friendship. Both cared about only one thing: winning the final to become the Shoot-the-Stairs Champion.

Lee watched keenly. He guessed that his brother would do something to give himself an advantage and he was right. Even before Joanne could complete the word 'two' Daz pushed himself off. He knew very well that no one had the power (or even cared enough) to order a re-start. All that mattered was being seen to be first past the post. Which he was by a wide margin. Somehow Daz mastered the necessary technique of keeping his balance while travelling at an almost uncontrollable speed round two severe bends; he didn't touch the banisters once. And when he came off his tray he turned a perfect somesault to show his glee.

'You cheated, you cheated!' accused Rupert when he reached ground level moments later.

'Rubbish!' Daz shot back predictably. 'In this game it's every man for himself. I did a fantastic time. Bet nobody'll beat it. And certainly not you, Lee-tle brother. Go on, then, let's see what you can do.'

Lee didn't beat his brother's time (or, at least, he didn't think he did: but as no one was using a stopwatch it was impossible to tell what times any of them were doing). Up against Greg, he knew that he'd have to be fast away to avoid being the victim of sharp practice. Like Darren, Greg would stop at nothing to get what he wanted in life. In a way, it was a pity they hadn't been drawn against each other.

In spite of his aggression and determination, Greg wasn't as boastful these days as he used to be and Lee supposed that was because the famed Shearsmith Special wasn't so successful nowadays: it had been superseded by the improved Honda and, now, the Namura. Greg's luck was out on the tray race, too. In spite of a flying start and a good line to the first turn he was unable to avoid the corner post – and the tray turned over, sending Greg tumbling down the stairs, a journey on which he was overtaken at speed by Lee, still comfortably seated. Lee breathed a sigh of relief. He'd been fearful Greg would eliminate him and thus allow Daz to crow once more about his family superiority.

To her intense delight Joanne defeated Adrian, despite taking a shuddering bump on the second bend which very nearly put her out of the race altogether. She was still ruefully rubbing her shoulder when Adrian very courteously came up to shake hands and congratulate her.

'Good job I was wearing shoulder pads,' she grinned. 'They bounced me back on to the track when I thought I was coming off altogether!'

'They're just for softies in this game,' scoffed Darren. 'You wouldn't get me putting 'em on. Slow you down, they do.'

Natalie was now busily organising the draw for

the semi-finals, a job Nathan said he'd supervise because Tally herself was one of the competitors and therefore 'you have to let everybody see that it's all completely fair.' Natalie didn't protest: she was excited by the prospect of winning the tournament and didn't mind who was in charge of the draw so long as they quickly got on with the racing. So far they'd been lucky in not attracting the attention of any adults but that situation might not last much longer, particularly as the actual races were quite noisy and spectators cheered on their favourites.

'Oh, terrific!' Natalie exclaimed when the draw was revealed. 'So it's bound to be a girl v. boy final. Sorry, Jo, but I'm going to be the one to get there.'

Darren shot a savage glance at his brother. 'And I'm going to be the other finalist,' he declared. 'Which means that I'll win the whole thing! No girl will stand a chance against me.'

Lee was having different thoughts. He'd been certain that the fates would pair him with Daz in the semi-final. So once again he was going to have to prove that he was the better rider. Whatever nasty tricks Daz might get up to (and he'd be sure to try something), Lee had to overcome them. In the race against Greg he'd been amazed by the speed he'd reached on the brake-less tray: the whole experience was as daring as it was dangerous. It felt as if he was defying death itself.

'Come on, then, kiddo, let's get going,' yelled

Darren, charging up the stairs for the first semi-final. 'Everyone can see you're scared to face me. Dead right. You haven't a hope!'

Lee was saving his breath and trying to work out the best route. Against Greg he'd stayed on the inside and that had worked in his favour. It might not against Daz. But Daz, by getting to the head of the stairs first, had already chosen the inner berth for himself, so that resolved the matter.

'Listen, you're got to wait for the proper signal,' called Nathan from the finishing point, he having now taken over the role of starter too. 'No jumping the gun, Darren. OK?'

'Get on with it,' replied Daz, making no promises.

Lee's grip tightened on the side of the red and gold tray, his right foot poised for the push start. Whatever happened, he *must* beat Daz.

'One, two – ' Nathan started to intone; and before he could utter another syllable both trays were on the move, with, if anything, Lee fractionally ahead. He'd known his brother was going to cheat and Lee decided he wasn't going to be his victim again.

Daz was enraged by that tactic. He knew that in the races so far not one rider had succeeded in overhauling another. So unless he took decisive action immediately he would lose his semi-final, lose to his *younger* brother again. It would be a failure he couldn't live with for even one minute. He made up his mind what to do.

With all the strength he could muster Darren wrenched his tray to the right, aiming to ram Lee amidships and knock him out of the contest.

But he miscalculated. It took him a few seconds longer than he thought it would to make the turn: and by the time he'd done it Lee had slipped further ahead. Instead of hitting his brother's tray Darren crashed, head-on, into the banisters.

The noise was like a series of minor explosions. Because, rebounding from the woodwork, Daz performed a couple of involuntary somersaults, landing first on one shoulder and then the other, before ending up in a sprawl just beyond the first bend in the staircase. As his brother's tray slithered down behind him Lee swiftly and serenely swept round the two turns and into the buffers at the finish. His arms shot up to signal his joy.

But it wasn't exactly a bloodless victory. For everyone was now staring up the staircase in consternation at the slumped figure of Darren Parnaby.

'Daz, you all right?' Nathan was calling out tentatively when Joanne, realising that something was seriously wrong, suddenly leapt past him, taking the stairs three at a time. If her cousin had taken only a slight knock he'd've been creating a terrible fuss about it; his complete silence told a different story.

Daz was struggling to his knees when Joanne

reached him, his face contorted with pain, his right arm reaching across to his left shoulder. His face was so white he didn't need to tell her how severe the pain was.

'I think I've broken it,' he muttered, leaning against her for support. If she hadn't held him he'd've fallen again.

'Can't be that bad – ' she was saying when the main door into the entrance hall opened and Mike Martin walked in. In the excitement of the races no one had been keeping watch and his arrival dumbfounded everyone.

'What the heck's going on here?' he demanded, trying to take in the entire scene in one raking glance. 'Have you lot been up to something stupid?'

'Look, we were just fooling around, that's all, nothing terrible,' said Natalie, taking the initiative again after a moment's stunned silence. 'Daz – Darren – has just had an accident – fallen – and seems to have hurt his shoulder.'

Now it was Mike who darted up the staircase to see what was wrong. One look at Daz's ashen face and the sweat beginning to bead his forehead was enough.

'We'd better get you to a doctor, son,' he decided. Then he changed his mind: 'No, the casualty department at the hospital would be better. You probably need an X-ray. Look, we'll go in my car.

D'you think you can manage to get down the stairs, Darren?'

'I'll try,' Daz said in a woeful voice.

Even before Mike Martin turned round to descend the staircase the cushions and the rugs and the serving tray Lee had ridden were out of sight. Natalie and Nathan had seen to that while some of the others were hiding the pads for knees and shoulders. Joanne was still supporting Daz but Lee didn't quite know what to do. He was sure Daz wouldn't want any help from *him*.

'Do you want me to come to the hospital with you, Mike?' Lee asked.

'Might be a good idea,' the promotions manager agreed. 'The rest of you had better start sorting yourselves out. I just called in to see how you were getting on and find you looking as guilty as a load of convicts. To say nothing of what's happened to Darren. When I get back I'll want to know the full story.'

They all trooped out on to the terrace to see Darren installed in the back of Mike's car. It would have been impossible for him to sit at the front and wear a seat belt.

'Hope everything turns out OK, Darren,' Natalie called but she didn't get a reply. Then, as soon as the car was out of sight, she turned to the rest of them and said: 'Right, I've been thinking things through. Here's our story. . . .'

# Eight:   Waiting to Pounce

For Lee, the sight of someone else riding a Namura motorcycle in the Taplow Castle Special Invitation Motocross was the second major shock he'd received in not much more than twelve hours. True, no one had ever told him he'd be the only rider competing on the exclusive Green Machine; he'd just assumed that because of all the attention he'd been given by Mike Martin and his promotions team.

'Who is that?' Lee asked Joanne who was already studying the official list of competitors that was on display in the window of the organiser's caravan by the paddock.

'Oh, 17,' she said, checking the race number on the bike. 'That's Finn Beanland. Natalie's heard of him and reckons he's a class performer. What's his nickname, now? Oh yes, the Flying Finn. Funny name, though, isn't it?'

'It's Irish, I think,' replied Lee, absently. Who, he was wondering, were Namura testing? Both of them? Or just him? Were they going to decide on the outcome of this race which of them should ride for Namura in future?

Until Finn Beanland literally rode into his view Lee had been feeling that things were going his way. Now that Darren was out of the race with a cracked collar-bone his fear of being ambushed again by his brother had gone. He could rely completely on his own skills as a rider and the power of the new bike. Now, however, he would be facing not only top class rivals but another Green Machine that would, presumably, be at least as good as his own.

'I must go and have a talk with Mike,' Lee was announcing when Joanne exclaimed: 'Oh dear, how awful. That boy over there by the hedge has just been sick. Hope he's not riding if he's ill.'

'That happens to lots of riders in this game – it's just nerves,' replied Lee fairly unconcernedly. 'You need iron stomach muscles to be a motocrosser, you know. That's why I went in for weight training and karate and that sort of thing, to get the whole body as fit as possible.'

'Oh yes, I suppose so,' murmured Joanne, still looking askance at the stricken rider. But, a couple of minutes later, he was re-united with his Kawasaki and jauntily talking to a friend.

Lee spotted Mike chatting to one of the officials and he hovered just out of earshot until they parted. The promotions manager greeted him with the sort of broad smile that hadn't been evident the previous evening when they took Daz to the local hospital. Clearly he'd been as worried about the injury as anyone and, naturally, he'd wanted to know how it happened. For once, Daz displayed some common-sense by saying the whole thing had been his fault: he'd been fooling around and fallen down the stairs. He hadn't implicated anyone else in the incident for which Lee was profoundly thankful. If Daz had told the truth then they could all have been banned from taking part in today's motocross. After receiving treatment Daz had been taken home by Uncle Ken who'd been summoned by a phone call from the hospital.

'Any news of the casualty this morning?' Mike wanted to know.

'Well, Uncle Ken phoned Mum this morning and Daz said he's still got a lot of pain – but he would say that. Daz is always terrible about his injuries even if he scratches his little finger. I think he's surviving, though.'

'And so are you, luckily,' Mike observed. 'You could have missed this race, Lee, after what was going on last night. I don't know the full story and I don't want to. But I have my suspicions. I just hope you all learnt a lesson. And I also hope you're going to reward me for my discretion by riding a blinder of a race today, Lee. I want to see a Namura taking the chequered flag. This is a top class event and I want us to dominte it. So, Lee, it's all up to you.'

Lee didn't see it quite like that. 'But there's another rider on a Namura. I thought I was the one who'd been chosen to demonstrate the bike's qualities. I mean, that's what you told us.'

Mike grinned and drove the fingers of his left hand through his hedge of gingery hair. 'Don't you think competition is healthy? Isn't that what motocross is all about? One guy racing to beat another?'

'Er, yes,' Lee had to agree.

'Well, two Namuras are therefore better than one. Maybe the sight of Finn Beanland's rear wheel will fire you up a bit more. He's a very fast starter is our Flying Finn.'

'I'm usually a fast gater myself,' Lee pointed out.

'Of course you are,' Mike nodded approvingly. 'By the way, have you cleaned your teeth today, Lee?'

'What?' Lee thought the Namura man had suddenly gone mad.

'The advertising from the toothpaste company you're displaying! I mean, if one of their reps is present he'll want to see that you're using the company's product, won't he? After all, this is a race to get your teeth into, isn't it?'

'Oh no!' Lee groaned at the feebleness of that joke.

'Glad to see you can still take a joke, Lee. Must say, you were looking pretty miserable a few moments ago. Got to dash now – hundreds of things still to see to. So have a good race – and keep Namura on the victory trail.'

Before Lee could move off to see to his bike Natalie collared him. 'Did Mr Martin say anything about last night?' she inquired anxiously.

Lee shook his head. 'Not really. He seems to have decided it's not worth going on about, that we won't do it again because of what happened to Daz.'

'Oh, great! But I'm glad we cleared everything up as fast as we did – and everybody was ready to swear we hadn't done anything really bad. I didn't want to miss the racing today. I mean, have you *seen* the trophies? Best I've ever seen, look like real silver most of them. Well, those for the winners, anyway. And that's what I'm aiming for, Lee. So watch out!'

Trophies were well down Lee's list of priorities at present. His first concern was to finish ahead of Finn Beanland and thus justify Mike Martin's faith in him as a regular Namura rider; winning the race was, on this occasion, of secondary importance. Because there were two of them riding Green Machines and the Namura girls were very active in drumming up public interest in Namura products Lee himself wasn't the centre of attention as he had been at Kingskettle. He had more time to think and plan what he was going to do.

As usual, he'd already walked the entire circuit on his own and so discovered just how formidable it was. The Castle grounds were so extensive that a metalled road bisected them, a road that the motocross circuit actually crossed at one point; that was going to be one of the chief hazards because from the tarmac the track plunged heart-thuddingly into a wooded zone. There it narrowed for a stretch of about three hundred metres along which it would be virtually impossible for two bikes to travel side-by-side. Bales of straw had been placed at the foot of the most obtrusive trees but projecting roots would be among the worst hazards.

The biggest obstacles of all, however, was the one the locals called The Wall. To Lee, as he stood back and stared at it for the first time, it resembled the face of a cliff: an almost vertical climb from a right-hand turn directly opposite an arched entrance to the castle grounds. So that ascent ran parallel to the high perimeter wall that surrounded the entire estate. If rider lost control on The Wall, or was in the wrong gear to climb it, then there was really no hope of recovery. Still, at least it didn't come up early in the race: there was time to prepare for it.

'All the best, then, you two,' Uncle Ken said as Lee and Joanne left the paddock together to make their way to the starting gate. The field was quite a small one: but then, as Nathan observed, 'It's only for the elite riders!' Because of his record with the clubs of which he was a member Finn was regarded by most as the favourite but Adrienne Tuff had a good reputation, too. Lee, who'd never met her before, was surprised by how small she was; from her name he'd expected her to be stocky and powerfully-built. On her Kawasaki she actually looked quite diminutive, almost bird-like. Balance and judgment of pace were her great attributes.

'Best of luck – especially at The Wall,' Lee called across to Joanne just before the visors came down and the roar of the engines built up.

'Oh, I was trying to forget that!' she gulped.

Lee had been drawn alongside the Flying Finn who was dressed, of course, in an identical outfit; only the advertising logos and panels were different. He had been warned about that flying start and he was determined to match it. So he felt he needed to keep one eye on his rival and the other on the starter. Sometimes it was possible to tell from the starter's change of expression or hand movement when he was going to give his signal.

Lee hadn't expected the starter to wink first. But Finn had – and that split-second advantage before the gate fell open allowed him to zoom away ahead of everyone. There was no time for Lee to feel annoyed by such cheating: pursuit was all that was in his mind. But Natalie had reacted even faster and it was her red and black Honda that was in second place when the field rounded the first left-handed

hairpin before climbing into the highest of the wooded sections.

Joanne was keeping as close as she could to Lee. Her father's advice was that this was a circuit on which it was impossible to win from way back, by trying to thread you way through the failures on the last couple of laps: you had to set the pace yourself or keep right up with the leaders. Well, not yet having acquired the gating skills of Finn and Lee, she had to be content with just a good start, not a brilliant one. But already she was ahead of such experienced sprinters as Rupe Hoyte and Stevie

Stranahan whose scarf today was a mixture of blues and yellows and seemed longer than ever.

Already there was the first casualty. Within the first 500 metres her bike split its rear spindle nut and shed the chain and so Adrienne Tuff, who had such high hopes of winning, was out of the race. It was no consolation at all to her to hear a spectator remark: 'Well, a girl as pretty as that oughtn't to be hiding her beauty under a helmet and those big goggles. She should be parading up and down as a model in the lastest fashions!'

The noise was like a swarm of angry wasps as the leading bunch of motocrossers reached the summit and then, with swift changes of gear and eager acceleration, headed downwards for some of the wilder terrain on the circuit. Natalie, believing that this was going to be her day, was crowding Finn at every turn.

Behind them, Lee and Joanne were comfortably holding off a challenge from Stevie and Rupe and, now emerging from the main cluster, Nathan Pike; so supporters of the Skalbrooke team had plenty to cheer about with so many of their riders in prominent positions. But sympathy was what Greg Shearsmith needed as he toiled at the rear of the field.

Soon there was one rival fewer for Lee to worry about. On that narrow stretch where trees hemmed in the riders Stevie, swerving to avoid a protruding

root, encountered exactly the kind of problem people had warned him about ever since he'd taken to
flaunting a scarf during racing. For the scarf
snagged on an overhanging low branch and the jerk
as it unravelled at speed threw Stevie completely off
balance – and he and his KTM parted company.
The bike smacked into a tree so fiercely that the
front wheel collasped; the rider was much, much
luckier because he landed on a straw bale.

He got to his feet immediately and saw, ruefully,
that the race was over for him; but when he caught
sight of the scarf, now dangling from the branch, he
realised how lucky he'd been. If it hadn't unwound
from his neck as fast as it did he'd have been
garotted, the fate he'd been told could await him if
he persisted in wearing it. He was thankful he could
still swallow all right: and he left the scarf where it
was as the warning that had now been heeded.

Lee was within a wheel's diameter of Natalie's
bike as they reached the end of that ribbon of a route
through the woods. He could sense, rather than see,
The Wall looming up and he knew it was vital to
approach the initial slope on precisely the right line.
He couldn't overtake Natalie on the left and so he
dropped back to take her on the right. He just hoped
she wouldn't falter and throw him off course.

But she did. Changing gear too sharply and
braking, she drifted across his path. Lee was forced
to pull over to the left. His momentum on the hill

was such that he had no alternative but to go round again in a wide sweep before he could face the gradient again at the right angle for the ascent. Lee muttered furiously at the loss of time and the advantage his good start had given him.

Natalie herself had stalled but both Joanne and Nathan had gone past him by the time Lee got to the top of The Wall: so from third place he'd dropped back to fourth just when he thought he as going to clinch second spot. At the next S-bend he took a quick check and saw that Natalie was now sixth, some way behind Adrian Linthwaite who was making stealthy progress. Rupe, attempting another of his rash slides in relief at scaling The Wall, had hit a barrier post and damaged the fork of his bike, putting him out of contention.

It took Lee several laps of concentrated endeavour to get into winning position again; but he was judging his line to perfection and saving metres on each circuit by every fractional adjustment as he took each twist and turn. The Green Machine responded magnificently to every demand he made of it and his confidence rose as high as The Wall itself, no longer an obstacle of terror to him.

There was also an element of luck in his success. First, Joanne was forced out of the race because of a wheel wobble which turned into a puncture caused by a hawthorn spike that had worked into the tyre (and had Lee been riding the Honda he, too, would have been out of the race through sheer misfortune). Then, with only a couple of laps to go and while Lee was pressing him hard, Nathan collided with the very root that Stevie'd been trying to avoid and that bounced him out of action. So now there was only Finn Beanland in front of him. The two Namuras were placed first and second: but which would win?

Now that he had the other Green Machine so clearly in his sights Lee had no doubt at all about the outcome. His strategy was simple: he would close the gap as quickly as possible and then sit on Finn's tail for a time. Talking with other riders in the paddock and with one of the Namura girls, Lee had learned that Finn hated to be harried. He couldn't bear to be stalked as a cat will stalk a mouse. So Lee, having made Finn aware of his presence by pulling out to ride alongside at one stage, now sat and waited . . . and waited. . . .

He waited only until they reached The Wall for the last time. And there he pounced, cutting into the hill from the most acute angle possible and so taking Finn by surprise. Fearing a collision, the leader veered away to the left – and his momentum was lost. Lee roared to the top of the incline, executing a giant leap as he regained level ground again: and now there was no one left to prevent him from completing a consummate victory, seconds ahead of the second Green Machine.

'Well, we couldn't have asked for anything better,

could we?' exulted Mike Martin, the first person to reach the victor and share in his great elation. 'You know, Lee, motocross success usually comes down to the flair of the individual. And that's where you certainly scored today. Great stuff. We're proud of you!'

Michael Hardcastle regularly visits schools and libraries around the country. If you would like to meet him, please ask your teacher or librarian to write to the address below:

MAMMOTH Press Office
Michael Hardcastle Visit
38 Hans Crescent
London SW1X 0LZ

# ROAR TO VICTORY

*Michael Hardcastle*

Lee Parnaby's main ambition in life – and one that he's determined to achieve – is to win the Intermediates' race of the Skalbrooke Schoolboy Motorcycle Club. His skill and bravery are without question. But when the big day comes will Lee's luck hold out?

# FAST FROM THE GATE

*Michael Hardcastle*

Lee Parnaby eats, breathes and sleeps motorbikes and motocross racing. When he tackles the downhill jump – the most dreaded hazard on the circuit – at top speed, he believes himself to be a winning scrambles rider. It's lucky for Lee that he can't foresee the desperate trouble ahead for him off the track: trouble which may mean that he never sees his bike again.

Full of suspense and drama on and off the racing track, *Fast From the Gate* is the sequel to *Roar to Victory*.

# A Selected List of Fiction from Mammoth

While every effort is made to keep prices low, it is sometimes necessary to increase prices at short notice. Mammoth Books reserves the right to show new retail prices on covers which may differ from those previously advertised in the text or elsewhere.

The prices shown below were correct at the time of going to press.

All these books are available at your bookshop or newsagent, or can be ordered direct from the publisher. Just tick the titles you want and fill in the form below.

**Mandarin Paperbacks**, Cash Sales Department, PO Box 11, Falmouth, Cornwall TR10 9EN.

Please send cheque or postal order, no currency, for purchase price quoted and allow the following for postage and packing:

| | |
|---|---|
| UK | 80p for the first book, 20p for each additional book ordered to a maximum charge of £2.00. |
| BFPO | 80p for the first book, 20p for each additional book. |
| Overseas including Eire | £1.50 for the first book, £1.00 for the second and 30p for each additional book thereafter. |

NAME (Block letters) ......................................................................................................................

ADDRESS ......................................................................................................................

......................................................................................................................

......................................................................................................................